SCLG
1-12
P9-APO-703

Sweet Persuasions

Rochelle Alers

THORNDIKE PRESS
A part of Gale, Cengage Learning

GALE
CENGAGE Learning™

Detroit • New York • San Francisco • New Haven, Conn • Waterville, Maine • London

Copyright © 2011 by Rochelle Alers.
An Eaton Summer Wedding Series.
Thorndike Press, a part of Gale, Cengage Learning.

ALL RIGHTS RESERVED
This is a work of fiction. Names, characters, places and incidents are either the product of the author's imagination or are used fictitiously, and any resemblance to actual persons, living or dead, business establishments, events or locales is entirely coincidental.
Thorndike Press® Large Print African-American.
The text of this Large Print edition is unabridged.
Other aspects of the book may vary from the original edition.
Set in 16 pt. Plantin.

LIBRARY OF CONGRESS CATALOGING-IN-PUBLICATION DATA

Alers, Rochelle.
Sweet persuasions / by Rochelle Alers. — Large print ed.
p. cm. — (An Eaton summer wedding series) (Thorndike Press large print African-American)
ISBN-13: 978-1-4104-4182-9 (hardcover)
ISBN-10: 1-4104-4182-2 (hardcover)
1. African Americans—Fiction. 2. Charleston (S.C.)—Fiction. 3. Large type books. I. Title.
PS3551.L3477S93 2011
813'.54—dc23 2011028172

Published in 2011 by arrangement with Harlequin Books S.A.

Printed in Mexico
1 2 3 4 5 6 7 15 14 13 12 11

Seek ye the Lord while He may be found,
call ye upon Him while He is near.

— *Isaiah* 55:6

Dear Reader,

The Eatons are back! So far, the setting has moved from Philly to D.C., and now we're moving to the sultry low-country.

When Xavier Eaton left Charleston after graduating with distinction from The Citadel, The Military College of South Carolina, his plans did not include returning and making The Holy City his hometown. The former career military officer is now a civilian, looking to begin the next phase of his life as a teacher at a small military academy.

What he doesn't plan on is falling in love. But when he walks through the door to Sweet Persuasions, it doesn't take much persuasion before he offers chocolatier Selena Yates his heart, protection and a love that promises forever.

Settle down in a comfortable chaise with a glass of sweet tea or lemonade and enjoy the heat, passion and a whirlwind romance that will not only leave you breathless, but panting for more.

The Eaton summer wedding duet continues

next month with Dr. Mia Eaton's *Sweet Destiny.*

Read, love and live romance.

Rochelle Alers

CHAPTER 1

Xavier Philip Eaton maneuvered into the empty parking space on King Street. The owner of one of the antiques shops lining the street had called him the day before to let him know that she'd been able to acquire some crystal and silver serving pieces from an estate sale, which he was thinking of giving his sister as a wedding gift. In less than three months, his sister Denise would be getting married and changing her last name from Eaton to Fennell.

He'd been as surprised as his parents were when Denise announced that she'd reconciled with her college sweetheart — after a six-year separation — and was marrying the successful Washington, D.C. businessman Garrett Fennell on New Year's Eve. When Xavier had asked his mother Paulette Eaton about a wedding gift, she'd suggested giving the couple something in keeping with the late-nineteenth-century architecture of their

D.C. town house. His future brother-in-law, Garrett, had purchased a four-story town house just blocks from the city's trendy, upscale Dupont Circle, renovating the first three floors for his various holding companies and the fourth floor as their personal residence. The renovations were scheduled to be completed before the end of the year, and Denise had decided to decorate the town house with period antiques and reproductions. Besides the wedding gift, he also had to buy something for his sister's upcoming birthday.

As the brother of the bride, Xavier was not only part of the ceremony, but he would have the honor of walking his sister down the aisle, since their father Judge Boaz Eaton had agreed to officiate. For the moment Denise's wedding had taken the pressure off of him, since his mother was obsessed with having her children get married and giving her grandchildren. It seemed Paulette Eaton was competing with her sister-in-law, Roberta Eaton, whose children had all married and made her a grandmother many times over.

Xavier wasn't against marriage, per se. It was just that he hadn't met a woman he wanted to spend the rest of his life with. Considering his former girlfriends, he could honestly say there hadn't been "one that got away." He'd been forthcoming with the women he'd dated, admitting that he wasn't ready to settle down and become a husband and father. And at the time, he wasn't certain where he'd wanted to go with his military career. Most of the women respected his honesty, and many of them had remained friends even after their relationship ended. Those who wanted marriage opted for a more permanent break.

In the past year, he had undergone major changes in his life. A combat injury had ended his military career, and he had moved back to Charleston, South Carolina for the second time in more than a decade. In college, he'd been a student at The Citadel, The Military College of South Carolina, where he'd graduated with distinction. He'd subsequently enrolled in The Citadel's graduate school, earning a degree in U.S. History and then went on to earn another degree at the Marine Corps War College. This time, he was back in Charleston not as a student, but as a teacher at a small, elite military prep school, teaching U.S. Military History. Just when he'd thought his days of wearing a uniform were over, he found out he still had to wear one whenever he was on campus.

It was late September, and the sultry heat of summer had not yet subsided. After growing up in Pennsylvania, he'd come to appreciate the relatively mild Southern seasons. Walking along King Street, he slowed his pace when he peered into the window of a pastry shop that displayed desserts and sweets reminiscent of a Parisian patisserie.

He smiled when he read the white lettering on the dark blue awning: Sweet Persuasions. The delectable confections were the pastry shop's best advertising. Xavier stared through the front window at the customers sitting at bistro tables, sipping espresso and noshing on savories and tarts. When he saw a sign indicating that shipping was available, he knew exactly what he'd get Denise for her birthday. He'd always thought of his sister as delicate when it came to desserts. She preferred chocolate éclairs and tiramisu to pound cake or peach cobbler.

He opened the door — painted a high-gloss, dark blue — and walked into the cool air-conditioned space. The soft tinkling of the bell just inside the door caught the attention of the young woman behind the counter. She offered him a friendly smile.

"Good morning. Welcome to Sweet Persuasions."

Xavier went completely still. Her voice was as enticing to his ear as the pastries in the window were to the eye. The sound of her voice was low, rich and ethereally melodic. The inflection had Charleston overtones, but not so much that he could detect exactly where she was from.

"Good morning," he said, reluctantly pulling his gaze away from the face that matched the hypnotic accent. If he had been asked to describe her, it would have been in the mouthwatering way one describes a confectionery masterpiece. Her face was the color of toasted hazelnuts, and her almond-shaped eyes were as dark as chocolate chips. He liked the way her nose crinkled when she smiled, but it was her mouth with its perfectly curved lips that garnered his rapt attention. His gaze shifted from the blue-and-white-checkered scarf tied around her hair to the trays of pastries, cookies and tarts.

"May I help you with something?" Xavier stood awestruck. "Sir?" she said, when he didn't respond.

"Oh, I'm sorry," he apologized. "Everything looks too pretty to eat."

Selena Yates felt her heart rate kick into a higher gear when she stared at the tall, slender man who'd walked into her pastry shop. She had lost count of the number of gorgeous men she'd seen since moving from West Virginia to Los Angeles and now Charleston, but the one standing before her literally and figuratively took the cake. He was more than delicious — he was scrumptious.

He wore a white polo shirt and khakis with the aplomb of a well-tailored suit. There was something in his ramrod-straight posture that commanded attention. Thick black eyebrows framed a lean reddish-brown face that lifted a fraction when their gazes met and fused. She found the deep dimples in his face breathtaking whenever he smiled. There was a tattoo on his inner right arm, but she wasn't able to make it out.

"Is there anything you'd like to sample?" she asked.

Xavier laughed heartily, the rich sound bubbling up from his chest. "I don't think you'd want me to do that," he said when he sobered.

Selena smiled. "Why not?"

He leaned in closer. "Because, I'd inhale everything in here like an anteater. I saw the sign said that you do shipping. Where?"

"We can ship our goods anywhere in the lower forty-eight."

"Overnight?" he asked.

"I can guarantee overnight if it's along the east coast. Otherwise, it'll be two-day delivery. Your order will be packed and sealed in a special container that is heat resistant, ensuring that it will be fresh by the time it arrives."

Smiling, Xavier continued to stare into the dark eyes that didn't seem to look *at* him as much as through him. "I'd like to send something to my sister in D.C. for her birthday. What would you suggest?"

"Is she allergic to chocolate or nuts?" Selena asked him.

It wasn't often that she had male customers. Most of her patrons were women who came into the shop to enjoy specialty coffees and teas with a pastry or savory tart, or to pick up an assortment of cookies or sweets for their offices, or to place an order for a special occasion. In the six months since the shop opened, Selena had been blessed because business was good. Some of her customers had standing orders, and her mail-order business had increased appreciably in the past few months.

Xavier shook his head. He pointed to a tray with cream-filled chocolate cookies. "She prefers sweets like these."

Selena peered into the showcase. "Those

are hazelnut galettes. They're chocolate rounds filled with *fromage frais,* a kind of cream cheese," she explained.

"Will they stay fresh during shipping?"

She wanted to ask him if he'd heard her when she'd mentioned the special shipping container. Flashing a smile usually reserved for children, Selena nodded. "If it arrives inedible, then I'll replace the order at no charge. By the way, they are usually served chilled."

Xavier moved along the length of the display case, his gaze lingering on the trays of brownies. "What kind of brownies are these?" he asked.

"Those are caramel-pecan." Selena reached for a pair of tongs and a napkin with her clear latex gloves. She picked up a brownie square, and handed it to Xavier. "Taste it."

He bit into the moist fudge, chewing slowly while shaking his head. "That's definitely X-rated," he drawled, after swallowing.

"The sweets in this showcase are what I call decadent delectables."

Xavier took another bite. "I take it back. It is triple-X-rated."

That's what Selena loved, someone who appreciated her variation on the classic brownie recipe. "Do you think your sister would like the brownies?"

"Yes." If there was one thing Xavier knew for certain, it was that Denise was a chocoholic. "She loves chocolate," he added.

Selena smiled. "Do you mind if I put together an assortment that I think she might like?"

"Please."

"I'll need you to fill out the shipping information." She pointed to a counter-height table with an empty stool in the corner. "The forms are over there. I'd appreciate it if you would sign the guestbook so that I can send you notices about our specials."

Reaching for his BlackBerry, Xavier scrolled through the directory for Denise's address. He filled out the shipping information, but decided it was best to send the package to her job instead of her apartment.

The coziness of the shop enveloped him as he hummed along with the soft music piped in through the speakers. Three couples sat at bistro tables, talking quietly as the tantalizing aroma of coffee filled the shop. Sweet Persuasions was exactly what the name implied. The subtle charm of the owner and the tantalizing pastries had drawn him in. But taste had been what sealed the deal. His gaze lingered on the raised lettering on the stack of business cards in a silver tray. A smile tilted the corners of his mouth. If the woman with the sensual voice behind the counter was the owner, then she had to be Selena Yates.

As he completed the shipping information, Xavier thought about his mother. Since she had retired from teaching, she'd begun baking in her spare time. Even though Paulette Eaton's cakes and cookies were delicious, they weren't as fancy or elaborate as those in Sweet Persuasions.

He picked up another shipping label. "I'd like another box like the one you're putting together."

Selena's hand stilled. "Is it going to the same address?"

"No. The other one is being shipped to Philadelphia."

"If you look in the drawer under the table, you'll see a choice of note cards and envelopes. Take the ones you want to accompany your orders."

Selena reached for a white box stamped with the shop's logo, filling it with brownies and miniature raspberry and peach almond cream tarts. She added two slices of a chocolate pecan torte and hand-rolled chocolate mocha candies filled with nuts and dried fruit.

She packed a smaller box with four one-ounce jars of homemade preserves: strawberry, plum-vanilla, blueberry-maple and peach. "All first-time customers receive homemade preserves as a gift," she told Xavier, as he stared at the tiny jars tied with blue-and-white ribbon.

"That's really nice," he crooned. He handed her the shipping forms.

Selena noticed that both labels were addressed to women with the same last name. She glanced at the return address. Now she had a name to go along with the face: Xavier Eaton. What she also noticed was that he lived in Charleston, so there was the distinct possibility that he would become a regular customer. Repeat business and local referrals had made Sweet Persuasions profitable.

"They'll go out today and they should receive them tomorrow."

Xavier took a small leather case from his pocket, and handed Selena a credit card. She stared at the plastic card. That's when he realized she was staring at the tattoo on his arm. He'd been tattooed twice. The first time was the Marine Corps insignia — a globe of the western hemisphere with an anchor through it and an eagle on top —

over his heart. He'd gotten the second tattoo after he was discharged.

As she took his credit card, Selena noticed that the image of a helmet resting on a rifle between a pair of boots, with the words *Never Forgotten* was the same as the one her brother had tattooed on one of his biceps.

Xavier's eyebrows lifted a fraction. "Does my tattoo bother you?"

Selena shook her head as she processed his payment. "No. My brother has the same one."

"Is he active?"

"No. He was in the reserves. But after two tours in Iraq, he decided it was time to get out. His wife threatened to divorce him if he didn't," she said, trying to avoid his gaze. "Are you active?"

Xavier exhaled an audible sigh. "No."

"Were you deployed?"

There came a moment of uncomfortable silence. "Yes," he finally said.

Selena felt the handsome stranger withdraw, even though the timbre of his voice hadn't changed. It was something she'd witnessed whenever her brother Luke had come home on leave. He'd spend hours locked in his bedroom, and when he'd emerged sometime later he was the brother she'd recognized from their youth — the practical joker.

"I'm sorry for prying."

Xavier forced a smile. "It's okay. You weren't prying."

If he hadn't worn a short-sleeved shirt, then she never would have seen the tattoo, he thought. He'd gotten it before the corps began cracking down on them. Suddenly, he seemed all too aware of it.

The carefree demeanor Selena had exhibited when he'd walked into Sweet Persuasions was now missing. "I'll be back to let you know whether my mother and sister enjoy them," Xavier said, hoping her smile and the cute way her nose creased would return.

"You can email me your comments."

He didn't know whether Selena Yates was married, single or engaged. But there was something about her that made him want to see her again. "I'll come by. Maybe next time I'll buy something for myself." She smiled, her eyes lighting up like a hundred-watt bulb. There were some people who smiled with their eyes or mouths, but with her it was both.

"Thank you, Mr. Eaton. I'd like that very much."

She could not afford to turn away any new

customer. She knew the risks of starting a new business, especially in a tough economy. But opening up a patisserie when she'd had no experience running a business at all defied common sense.

"It's Xavier," he corrected.

Selena extended her hand. "And I'm Selena."

He took her hand, holding it gently between his much larger one. "It's nice to meet you, Selena." Reluctantly he released her delicate fingers. "I'll be seeing you." Turning on his heels, Xavier walked to the door, standing aside to let a petite, dark-skinned woman with chin-length twists enter.

"Thank *you,*" she crooned seductively.

"You're welcome," he said, chuckling under his breath as he closed the door.

Monica Mills pirouetted in a pair of flats before bowing gracefully. "Now *that* looks as delicious, maybe even better, than what you're selling," she said to Selena.

Selena smiled at her next-door neighbor. "He's definitely eye candy."

Not only was Monica her neighbor, but they were also friends. Monica helped out in the shop during her free time, while Selena looked after the single mother's school-age daughter before and after school hours.

"I'll be right back," Monica said over her shoulder as she walked toward the kitchen at rear of the shop. She washed her hands, and then pulled a bib apron over her head tying it around her waist. She covered her hair with a nylon bouffant cap, pushing the wealth of neatly twisted hair under the elastic band.

Monica worked for a major Charleston law firm as a paralegal, and there were times when she didn't leave the office until well past seven o'clock, which is why Selena Yates was such a lifesaver.

Selena made certain Monica's daughter, Trisha, got on and off the school bus, completed her homework and fed her dinner. Selena refused to accept payment for babysitting Trisha, so Monica helped out at Sweet Persuasions. For the past month, she'd put in sixteen-hour days at the law firm because of a high-profile murder case that was scheduled to go to trial soon. So she'd decided to take two weeks off in lieu of overtime payment. No amount of money could take the place of her spending time with her eight-year-old daughter.

Selena was cradling the boxes to her chest when Monica emerged from the rear of the shop. "Please take care of the front, while I get these ready for the early pick up." A courier from the shipping company came twice a day — before noon and at six. A morning pickup ensured next-day delivery and the afternoon was for two-day deliveries.

"No problem, boss."

Selena rolled her eyes at Monica, who'd put off going to law school when she'd discovered a week before graduating from college that she was pregnant. Rather than tell her boyfriend he was going to be a father, Monica moved from Atlanta to Charleston to be closer to her family. When Selena had asked her neighbor why she hadn't told the man with whom she'd had a four-year relationship that she was pregnant with his child, Monica had said she didn't want to talk about it. Respecting her privacy, Selena never asked again.

"I'm not paying you, Ms. M. So, I'm not your boss."

Monica mimicked Selena's eye-rolling. "I should be the one paying you for all you do for Trisha."

Trying to avoid a pointless argument with her friend, Selena walked into the back of the shop. When she decided to open Sweet Persuasions, she'd had the contractor divide the space in the rear into a kitchen and a small alcove that she'd set up as an office. A desktop computer, printer, a two-drawer file cabinet and shelves stocked with boxes and shipping supplies was the mail-order lifeline of Sweet Persuasions. The kitchen where she baked her goodies was the heart and soul of the patisserie.

Selena gift-wrapped the boxes and attached gift cards. Forty-five minutes later, Xavier Eaton's bakery goods were wrapped and sealed in vacuum packaging and stored in containers of dry ice. She printed out the shipping labels, affixed them to the packages and placed them on a side table with three other orders.

When Selena had left West Virginia at eighteen to attend college in California, she never imagined that eight years later she would be running her own business. In less than three weeks, she would be celebrating her twenty-seventh birthday. And although she didn't know why, she suddenly felt older. Not old, but older. Becoming a pastry chef hadn't been her career choice at first. But spending hours making mouthwatering recipes for delicious desserts and candies had become her passion. She didn't have a husband, children or even a boyfriend, so her time was hers and hers alone.

Glancing at the wall calendar, she studied the requests for the upcoming week. There were orders for three dozen red-velvet cupcakes for a ladies auxiliary meeting, a specialty cake for a North Charleston couple celebrating their fiftieth wedding anniversary and a Black Forest cherry cake for an engagement party. Closing Sweet Persuasions two days a week allowed Selena to fill those special orders.

The nightmare that had sent her fleeing California to South Carolina was now a distant memory. Living and working in Charleston was like being reborn. She didn't have to look over her shoulder every time she left her house, or glance through the peephole whenever the doorbell rang.

She'd claimed a new city and state as her home. She had a new career and had set up a new business. Not only did Selena think her of herself as lucky — she believed she was blessed.

A hint of a smile softened Xavier's lips as he strolled out of Sweet Persuasions and down the block to the antiques shop. The past four months had become a summer of firsts. He had purchased his first house and he'd become a teacher.

He'd had second thoughts about relocating to Charleston after accepting the teaching position. But now that he'd moved into his house and settled into teaching military history, he felt as if he'd come home. Xavier was also rediscovering his adopted city — a city with a troubled past and a bright future.

He opened the door to the antiques shop, glancing at the unorthodox greeter sitting on a perch and staring at him from inside a large birdcage. "We have a visitor," squawked the colorful parrot. "What's your name?"

"Willie, I've told you about asking people their names," admonished a woman with fashionably coiffed hair the color of moonlight. The elegantly attired shopkeeper smiled at Xavier. "Good morning, Mr. Eaton. You're going to have to forgive Willie this morning. It's as if he's forgotten his home training."

"He's forgiven," Xavier mumbled under his breath.

He wanted to tell Charlotte Burke that her pet needed more than home training. Willie needed to be *at* home. The first time he'd visited the shop he was treated to a monologue peppered with salty language that left Mrs. Burke red with embarrassment.

Charlotte Burke sighed. She'd given Willie

a lengthy lecture as soon as she'd removed the cover from the cage earlier that morning. Her scolding had continued while she cleaned the cage and gave the parrot food and water. Willie had learned his colorful language from her husband, who claimed he could say whatever he wanted within the confines of his home. What Walter Burke had refused to acknowledge was that although there were no small children in the house, the parrot repeated everything he said.

She smiled at the incredibly gorgeous man, who made her wish that she was at least thirty years younger so she could flirt with him. Fortunately for her, she was married, and she wasn't a cougar like some of her friends.

"You're not teaching today?"

Xavier pulled his gaze away from what had become a stare down with the foulmouthed bird. Charlotte Burke's cornflower-blue eyes matched her pantsuit exactly. The strand of South Sea pearls around her neck coordinated with the pearl studs in her ears. Her face, unlike her hands, was wrinkle-free, leading him to believe she'd had some work done.

"Today's a school holiday."

The Christopher Munroe Military Academy, a college preparatory school for grades eight through twelve, had opened its doors to day and boarding students ninety years ago with just fourteen young men. The school's population had changed dramatically over the years with the acceptance of students of color and females, expanding to include grades one through twelve.

"That is so nice," Charlotte crooned, her Southern drawl more pronounced than usual. She pressed her palms together. "If you come with me, I'll show what I picked up at the estate sale."

Xavier followed her to a table with a collection of silver and crystal pieces. "How old is this one?" He'd pointed to a heavily decorated silver teapot.

Reaching for a square of felt, Charlotte handed him the pot. "It was made by Samuel Kirk & Son in the mid-nineteenth century. Throughout the late nineteenth-century Kirk specialized in flatware and hollowware with heavy repoussé work or chasing that resembles neo-Rococo. If you turn the pot over you'll see that it's signed."

"What is *chasing?*" he asked.

"It is a surface decoration drawn on the piece and then the decorator hammers it with a blunt, ballpoint chisel to distort the surface to achieve the desired effect without removing any metal."

"Amazing," Xavier said in a quiet voice. He set the teapot on the table, and picked up a coffeepot.

"That one is a silver Hallmark English coffeepot. It was made around 1767."

"I'll take the coffeepot, the teapot and the matching service pieces."

Charlotte nodded, staring at the length of lashes touching the top of Xavier Eaton's cheekbones. "What about the crystal?" She was hoping to sell him most of the silver *and* the crystal.

Reaching into a back pocket of his slacks, he took out a credit card. "I'm not sure what crystal pattern my sister would like, so I'm going to pass on it. But I know for certain that she's partial to silver."

"You've selected some very fine pieces." A slight frown appeared on Charlotte's face. "Didn't you tell me you're a history teacher?"

"Yes." Xavier had had a lengthy conversation with her when he'd first visited her shop. She was aware that he'd graduated from The Citadel, and that he'd returned to Charleston to teach part-time at a military school. A smile parted her lips, the gesture reminding him of a Cheshire cat.

"I have something I believe would be of

interest to you."

His eyebrows lifted a fraction. "What is it?"

"You'll see," Charlotte said in singsong voice.

His curiosity piqued, Xavier watched as the antiques dealer put on a pair of white-cotton gloves and placed a leather pouch on the table. She took out a tattered cloth-bound journal and then another that was equally worn. "These are the journals written by a freeman of color who fought with the Union army in the War Between the States."

He wanted to correct Mrs. Burke by telling her that the official term was the Civil War, but knew that the Confederate loss was a sore point with most Southerners. She opened the journal, turning the pages as if she were handling a newborn. Some of the entries were written in pencil and others in ink. Incredibly, most of the writing was legible.

Xavier leaned over the table. "If you don't mind my asking, where did you get these?"

Charlotte gave him a sidelong glance. "I found them."

"You just happened to find journals that are more than one hundred fifty years old?"

A flush suffused the woman's face. "I

really didn't find them. But, I promised the woman who gave them to me that I wouldn't divulge her name. She was cleaning out her house and she found them in a trunk in her attic. The trunk belonged to the great-grandmother of a woman who used to clean her grandmother's house."

Xavier tried to process what he'd just been told. "Why did she give them to you rather than a museum or historical society?"

Charlotte's flush deepened. "She said the memories were too painful and she just wanted them out of her house."

Realization dawned for him. Journals, if authenticated, that could be worth five or six figures at auction were given away like a bundle of old newspapers. "How much do you want for them?"

"I can't sell them."

A shiver of annoyance snaked its way up Xavier's back. "If you don't intend to sell them, then why show them to me?"

"That's because I want to give them to you."

He went completely still. "Do you have any idea what these are worth?"

Charlotte shook her head. "No, and I don't want to know. You teach history, Mr. Eaton, so I know you will make certain they will find a good home."

Xavier leaned forward. "You trust me not to sell them?"

"I've lived long enough to believe I'm a good judge of character. And I know you won't sell them because you'd want to share what's in these journals not only with your students but anyone interested in *our* country's history."

Charlotte Burke was right. He wouldn't sell the journals because he wasn't the rightful owner. Perhaps if he'd inherited or purchased them, then Xavier would possibly consider donating them to the South Carolina Historical Society. He planned to read the entries and then verify the accuracy of the events. After having them appraised, he would look for the rightful owner or owners. It was only fair that the descendants of a man who'd chronicled a war in which brothers took up arms against one another should be aware of what he'd had to sacrifice.

"You're going to donate them, aren't you?" Charlotte asked.

Xavier smiled. "I will — but only if I can't find the rightful owners. That shouldn't be too difficult if they're still living in South Carolina."

"What if they've moved out of the state?"

"It will make the search a bit more difficult, but not impossible. Did the lady tell you how long it had been since the woman cleaned her grandmother's house?"

Charlotte slipped the books into the leather case and removed her gloves. "No. I would've asked, but she appeared very upset. You would've thought she'd found a live snake in her house instead of century-old books."

What, Xavier mused, was her connection to the man who'd written of his wartime exploits? It had been a while since something had fired his imagination, and he was looking forward to what was certain to become a research project.

"If you don't mind, I'd like you to hold on to the journals until I come back. I have some more shopping to do. Meanwhile I'll pay you for the silver."

"But, we haven't negotiated a price, Mr. Eaton."

Xavier waved his hand in dismissal. "I don't like haggling. Please let me know how much I owe you."

Charlotte took umbrage to the term *haggling,* but dismissed it with a slight lifting of her shoulders. Haggling was for peddlers, not a professional antiques dealer such as herself. Xavier's willingness to meet whatever price she'd quote spoke volumes. He was a man willing to pay for whatever he wanted. She completed the transaction, processing his credit card and returning it to him. "My assistant will be in within the hour and, if you want, she can gift wrap them for you."

Xavier smiled and deep lines appeared along his lean jaw. "I would really appreciate that." And for the second time that day, he'd filled out a gift card to his sister. Six years older than Denise, he had always assumed the role of her protector. He'd put the word out in their neighborhood that if anyone bothered Denise Amaris Eaton, then they'd have to deal with him. Of course, he hadn't had to deal with bullying or fighting, since it wasn't tolerated in military school. Anyone who broke the rules was dealt with immediately. Three infractions in a school year meant permanent expulsion.

Xavier left the shop, skirting a couple standing in front of a shoe store, and headed for a specialty shop featuring tailored menswear. His day off had come with surprises. He'd discovered Sweet Persuasions and he had come into possession of a valuable piece of Civil War history.

CHAPTER 2

Selena adjusted the thermostat on the air-conditioning unit in the bedroom, sank down into a rocking chair, kicked off her shoes, propped her feet on a footstool and closed her eyes. She never realized how tired she really was until she sat down at the end of the day. Once she'd made the decision to open up the shop, it wasn't the decisions about which pastries she should make for her customers that had caused her so many sleepless nights. But it was the days and hours of running the business and the worries about money that were so exhausting.

Originally she'd considered staying open six days a week, but that would have left her little or no time to herself. In the end she decided to remain open Tuesday through Friday 8:00 a.m. to 6:00 p.m. She closed at four on Saturdays to keep her standing appointment to get her hair and nails done. Sundays were relegated to cleaning her apartment, doing laundry and attending church services. Mondays were set aside for banking and baking.

Selena opened her eyes, and stared at the bedroom furnishings she'd chosen as meticulously as she decorated the cookies and truffles displayed in Sweet Persuasions' showcase. As a girl she had always wanted to become an interior decorator, but that dream changed when she was bitten by the acting bug. Performing on stage and in front of cameras became her passion. But her world was shattered when she had to give up her acting career after her life was threatened.

It wasn't often Selena thought about what she'd sacrificed to start over, but retreating to the two-bedroom apartment above the shop that had become her sanctuary made it all worthwhile. Cloistered in her bedroom, she was able to relax and sleep in comfort *and* in peace.

The sound of the telephone ringing interrupted her musings. She picked up the cordless receiver without looking at the caller ID display — something she wouldn't have done when she lived in California.

"Hello."

"Hey, you."

Selena smiled upon hearing her sister-in-law's greeting. "Hey, Christy. How are you?"

"Pregnant!"

Her heart jumped. She knew her brother and his wife had been trying to have a baby, and after more than ten years of marriage Keith and Christine had begun talking adoption. "No!"

"Yes, and with twins."

"I can't believe I'm going to become an aunt."

"If everything goes well, then you'll become a double aunt."

"When is the baby . . . I guess I should say when are the *babies* due?" Selena asked.

"March fifteenth."

Selena calculated that Christine was approximately twelve weeks into her pregnancy. She found it odd that when she'd spoken to her mother, Geneva Yates, she hadn't mentioned she was going to be a grandmother. Perhaps, she mused, her brother and sister-in-law didn't want to say anything until after the first trimester.

"Do you know the sex of the babies?" she asked.

A soft chuckle came through the earpiece. "One looks like a boy, but the doctor couldn't tell about the other one."

"Perhaps you'll get one of each."

"That would be nice," Christine crooned.

"Enough talk about me. How's business?"

Staring at the rose color on her pedicured toes, the corners of Selena's mouth tilted upward when she smiled. "Business is better than I'd anticipated, especially the mail orders."

"Maybe one of these days you'll be a completely mail-order business."

"Maybe," she said, noncommittally. Sweet Persuasions had only been open for six months and that wasn't long enough to go from retail to exclusively mail order.

"Business is good, but what about you?" Christine questioned. "Are you seeing anyone?"

"I don't have time to see anyone," Selena said much too quickly.

"Yeah, right," Christine snorted. "Even the president and first lady have date nights."

She didn't want to talk about her lack of a love life since she'd moved from Los Angeles to Charleston. "You're right, Christy. Maybe now that Sweet Persuasions is doing well I'll think about accepting an occasional date or two."

"Don't you dare get sarcastic with me, Selena Yates."

Selena chatted with her sister-in-law for the next ten minutes and hung up. She always enjoyed talking to Christy, because just hearing her voice reminded her of home. It had been a long time since she'd been to West Virginia. She decided she needed to relax and decided to take a leisurely bubble bath.

After her bath, she planned to prepare a salad to go along with the leftover beef stew, watch an hour or two of television before going to sleep. Her life had become as predictable as the sunrise. Every day she left her apartment in the morning to go to the shop, and then back home again in the evening. It was becoming a routine, but more important, it was safe — safer than it had been in L.A. before she'd been forced to leave when her ex-lover became a stalker. If Derrick Perry hadn't been the son of one of California's most powerful political power brokers, he would've been in jail.

When she left L.A., Selena didn't go to West Virginia because she knew that would be the first place Derrick would look for her. Whenever she did go home, for holidays and family get-togethers, her father or her brothers would always pick her up at the airport. And because her father was in law enforcement, he always carried a handgun.

Her decision to move to Charleston wasn't capricious, but rather something she'd given a great deal of thought. With a population of more than one hundred twenty thousand, Selena knew she would be able to blend in easily in South Carolina's second-largest city. It was a Southern city, which better suited her temperament, making her feel more at home than she had in California. What she never imagined is that at twenty-six years old, she would be forced to change careers and start her life all over again in a new place. In Charleston, Selena had been give a second chance and she intended to take advantage of what the future held.

Xavier stood ramrod straight, his hands clasped behind his back, in the front of the classroom, meeting the curious eyes of the students in his class. Twenty years ago he'd been one of those students. He'd joined the faculty at Christopher Munroe Military Academy as a temporary instructor. The teacher he'd replaced was currently on medical leave and expected to return to the military academy the next school year. Xavier had accepted the position to get some teaching experience.

He hadn't known why he'd become obsessed with military life. But at the age of seven he'd asked his father whether he could go to military school. It had taken one day for Boaz to discuss it with his wife, and a month later Xavier went from a suburban Philadelphia public school to a military academy in a nearby town. Many of the cadets were there because of disciplinary problems. But there were some who, like Xavier, had taken to the rigid structure like a duck to water.

Knowing what to expect from the time he woke until he went to bed provided a certain comfort and sense of order. There was no gang violence. No competing with other boys for a girl's attention and on-campus substance abuse did not exist.

Unfolding his hands, he crossed his arms and smiled at the students seated in a semicircle. With a student-faculty ratio of eight-to-one, he much preferred the more informal seating arrangement to the usual classroom setup. All Munroe cadets wore uniforms, which helped foster a sense of camaraderie and put all the students on equal footing, giving them a chance to excel and be recognized.

"The Civil War marked a change in military warfare in this country that had been in place from the American Revolution to 1861."

"Was it because of weaponry?" asked a female cadet.

Turning toward the front of the classroom, Xavier picked up a marker and jotted down the word *artillery* on the board. "The technological advancement in weapons was a key factor. But remember, weaponry is used in all wars — whether it's pitchforks, axes, knives, swords, bows and arrows, bayonets, guns or cannon fire. Can anyone tell me about communications during this time?"

He was met with blank stares. Xavier enjoyed teaching the military course because it forced students to think. He'd set up a large storyboard with blue and gray toy soldiers. The rendering included mountain ranges, rivers, streams, seaports and railroads. He'd also pinned maps of the Americas, dating from the seventeenth century to the present on two of the four walls.

A rosy-cheeked boy glanced at his classmates and then raised his hand. "Had coded messages become more sophisticated?"

"In what way had they become more sophisticated, Mr. Lancaster?" Xavier responded.

"Spies no longer hid orders or maps in their boots," Cadet Lancaster announced proudly.

"Where would they hide them?" asked the other female cadet, this one sporting neatly braided hair she'd tucked into a twist on the nape of her neck.

"That is a good question, Ms. Jenkins," Xavier said, pausing before he wrote the word *telegraph* on the board, underlining it. "With every war there are intelligence officers, or as they are commonly referred to — spies."

Valerie Jenkins gestured for permission to speak. "I read the other day that if Major John André, who conspired with Benedict Arnold during the Revolutionary War, had been dressed as a soldier when he was captured, he would've been treated as a prisoner of war and not a spy."

Xavier was hard-pressed not to show how impressed he was with Valerie's eagerness to learn. "You're right. As a student of history, I've always wondered why Benedict Arnold would give André papers, written in his own handwriting, papers detailing how the British could take West Point when the British general already knew the fort's layout."

"Do you think General Arnold set up André, Major Eaton?" Valerie asked.

Xavier angled his head. "We'll never know. Major André sealed his own fate when he encountered a group of armed militiamen near Tarrytown, New York, assuming they were Tories because one man was wearing a

Hessian soldier's overcoat. He'd asked them if they belonged to the lower party, meaning the British, and they'd said they did. Then the major told them he was a British officer and he wasn't to be detained. Imagine his shock when the men told him they were Americans and he'd become *their* prisoner. The men searched him, found the papers and he was detained as a spy. He'd asked to be executed by a firing squad, but the rules of war dictated that he be hanged.

"Fast forward eighty years and Americans are embroiled in another war — this one unlike any other fought on this soil because it was not an invasion. Widespread use of the telegraph for military communications began with the Civil War. The telegraph wire service was a private enterprise, but its operators were affiliated with the U.S. Army. Using his executive power, President Lincoln put it under federal jurisdiction reporting to the War Department."

Another cadet raised his hand. "Yes, Mr. Tolliver," Xavier said, pointing to him.

"Major Eaton, are you saying Confederate troops didn't have access to the telegraph?"

"No, I'm not. Operators on both sides became adept at taping enemy lines and decoding messages, but the Confederates lacked the infrastructure of Union telegraphers who had more than fifteen thousand miles of telegraph wire and sent approximately six million military telegraphs." He made a notation next to artillery. "The Minié ball, or minie ball, is a muzzle-loading, spin-stabilizing rifle bullet that came into prominence during the Civil War. Like the musket ball, the minie ball produced terrible wounds. The large-caliber rounds easily shattered bones, and in many cases the field surgeons amputated limbs rather than risk gangrene. The result was massive casualties. The Spencer repeating carbine and rifle and Colt revolver rifle also played a major part when it came to artillery."

Xavier added photography, newspaper clippings, letters from soldiers, the railroad, transport troops and supplies, water transportation, topography and the science of embalming to the syllabus.

"The discovery that by combining arsenic, zinc and chloride to prevent bodies from decaying so quickly, meant that soldiers could be shipped home for burial rather than in mass graves. I want you to research each of these points and become familiar with their impact on the war for both the Union and Confederate armies."

Cadet Valerie Jenkins raised her hand

again. "There is no comparison when the Union Army controlled the telegraph lines."

"Are you saying, Cadet Jenkins, that the Confederates were completely inept when it came to communications? And if they were, why then did the war last four years?"

She lifted her shoulders. "I don't know."

Xavier smiled. "That's what I want you to find out. All of you have textbooks and access to the internet. Please use them. Remember, we're going to cover every battle and skirmish beginning with the opening salvo of the shelling of Fort Sumter in Charleston Harbor on April 12, 1861 to Lee's surrender at Appomattox April 12, 1865. You may think the issues I listed are inconsequential. But because of them battles were won and lost, heroes were revered and vanquished. Most of you have heard of the battles at Vicksburg, Lookout Mountain, Fredericksburg, Gettysburg, Bull Run and Manassas. But there was also Mechanicsville, Sailor's Creek, Missionary Ridge, Strasburg, Philippi, Rich and Cedar Mountain. We will go over military tactics and strategies from the point of view of both armies. What we will not discuss is the political or the moral implications of the war."

He glanced at the wall clock. "You have

fifteen minutes to copy the notes on the board." The cadets opened their laptops, waited for them to boot, then began typing. Unlike some instructors, Xavier preferred his students not take notes during the lecture because it was a distraction. He wanted them to absorb as much information as possible before transferring it to their notes. Times truly had changed since he'd attended military school. Yes, there were computers, but not every cadet had their own laptop.

Xavier dismissed the class. He knew the cadets were anxious to start the weekend. Having the next two days off let them blow off some steam. Come Monday morning the rigorous military education would begin again. And it wasn't the first time Xavier thought he was grateful he didn't live on campus. Once he'd received his official discharge from the marines, he was a civilian now living the life of a civilian. He was well aware that the transition from almost three decades in a military to civilian life wasn't going to be easy. But teaching at a military academy had made it easier.

A knock on the classroom door caught his attention. He looked up. "Have a good weekend, Major Eaton."

Xavier nodded to an instructor who taught

mathematics at Munroe. "Thank you, Captain Alston. You do the same."

For Xavier, every weekend was good, because for the first time in his adult life he would be able to go home and do whatever it was he wanted to do. He was no longer Captain Xavier P. Eaton, a rank he'd held for years before his promotion to major. The promotion had come when he'd risked his life to save three of his men who'd been wounded when they tripped an improvised explosive device — or IED. He'd managed to save two of them. After a month in a military hospital, where he was awarded a purple heart and another medal for bravery, Xavier was promoted to the rank of major, followed by several weeks in a rehabilitation facility that led to his medical discharge.

There were days when the pain in his leg had been so intense it made walking difficult. But he managed to work through the discomfort in order to maintain a relatively normal lifestyle. He'd gone from wheelchair to walker and eventually to walking with a cane. It had been more than two months since he'd used the cane he'd stored in the trunk of his car. Although he knew it would be some time before he'd be able to jog or run laps around a track, his orthopedist had assured him that there would come a time when he'd forget that rods, pins and screws had replaced his shattered bones.

Xavier walked out of the classroom and into the office he shared with two other history instructors, unlocked the drawer to his desk and retrieved his cell phone. He had two voice mail messages: one from his mother and another from his sister. He listened to his voice mail, smiling when he heard Paulette Eaton's message:

"Thanks so much for the incredible box of goodies. I shared them with Roberta who couldn't stop talking about them. She'd asked me whether I'd made them, and I couldn't lie. But I didn't tell her where I'd gotten them from, which truly made my day. Call me when you get a free moment. Love you."

Xavier shook his head as he scrolled through the directory for his sister's number. He wanted to tell his mother to give up her pointless undeclared war with her sister-in-law. The sooner Denise made their mother a grandmother, the better.

He hit the speed dial for New Visions Childcare, identifying himself and requesting to be connected with Denise Eaton. Her voice came through the earpiece less than sixty seconds later.

"What's up, brother love?"

A rich chuckle greeted her response. "I think it's Rhett who's brother love."

"Now, don't tell me you're not seeing anyone?" asked the director of the D.C.-based childcare center.

Xavier sobered. "I'm not seeing anyone. Does that satisfy your curiosity?"

"For now," Denise quipped. "What I can't understand, Xavier, is that you've been involved with some really nice women."

"Nice doesn't translate into special, Denise."

"How special is special?"

"I can't explain it. But I'll know when I meet her."

"Does she exist?"

He smiled even though his sister couldn't see his expression. "Of course she exists."

"Yeah, right," Denise drawled. "I want to thank you for the wonderful birthday gift. It was delivered minutes before this morning's staff meeting, so I shared them with everyone. Preston and Chandra invited me and Rhett to hang out with them for a couple of days, so I want to order something from Sweet Persuasions and have it delivered directly to them."

"That shouldn't be a problem," he told his sister.

"Will they deliver to the Brandywine Valley?"

"I suppose they will. It may be a little remote compared to Philly, but it is on the map." His cousin Chandra had married award-winning playwright P.J. Tucker, who owned a condo in Philadelphia's Rittenhouse Square and a farmhouse in the historic Brandywine Valley.

"Can you please go to the shop and check it out for me, Xavier?"

"You have the telephone number. Why don't you call?"

"I've been calling, but all I get is a busy signal."

He smothered a groan. "When do you need to know?"

"Like yesterday. We're leaving tonight, and plan to stay through Wednesday."

His plans included going home and unwinding. "Give me the Brandywine address and telephone number." Reaching for a pen, he wrote it down, repeating it to make doubly sure.

"I'll send you a check if you order —"

"Don't worry about sending me anything," Xavier said, interrupting her.

"But I want —"

"I don't want to discuss it, Denise. Save your money. Remember, you're the one planning a wedding."

"Have you forgotten your future brother-in-law is a multimillionaire?"

"And have you forgotten that it's the bride's family that usually pays for the wedding? So if you mention money to me again, I'm going to hang up on you."

"Damn, brother. There's no need to get hostile."

Xavier ignored her. "What do you want me to order?"

"I'd like a brownie-fudge cheesecake and a pound of chocolate-and-peanut-butter pretzels. I found out from Preston that Chandra has been craving chocolate and cheesecake."

"No comment." He knew any reference to food and a woman's weight was certain to set off an argument, so he made it a habit to remain silent on the subject. Chandra, who was due to deliver her first child a month after the wedding, had been chosen matron of honor. "I'm going to hang up because I want to go home and change before going into town. I'll call you later."

"Thank you, Xavier. You're the best brother a girl could have."

"Is it because I'm the only brother you have?"

"That, too," she said, laughing.

He ended the call, and put his cell phone into the leather case along with his laptop and lesson plans. Going downtown to order and ship pastries wasn't how he'd planned to begin his weekend. He managed to stave off his curiosity about the journals Charlotte Burke had given him until later. Once he sat down to read them, he didn't want any interruptions. He planned to read the entries and also take notes. As a student of American military history, he would know if details of the battles were accurate or not. But first he had to stop by Sweet Persuasions and place another order for his sister. There wasn't anything he wouldn't do for Denise. Memories of her crying whenever he returned to school after spending the weekends with his family had remained with him for hours. It had been impossible to explain to a toddler that her older brother wasn't deserting her, and that he would return home the following weekend to play with her.

It wasn't until Denise enrolled in school herself that she understood what her brother did when he went away to school. The guilt had bothered him for years. Ever since then he was helpless upon seeing a woman cry. It was the reason he'd remained friends with some of his former girlfriends. If they called to ask whether he would escort them to a social event he always agreed. That's what friends were for.

Returning to Charleston meant starting over for Xavier. It wasn't about looking for a woman as much as it was discovering who he was. For years he'd been a cadet, a first and then second lieutenant, captain and eventually a major. In Charleston, and away from military school, he could be Xavier Eaton — someone not bound by rules and regulations.

He left Munroe through a side door, leading directly into the faculty parking lot. Ninety minutes after driving away from the academy he maneuvered onto a side street behind Sweet Persuasions. Crews and trucks from a utility company had blocked off King Street to cars. It was apparent they were there to restore telephone service to the area.

Xavier walked around the corner and when he approached the shop with the blue awning he saw Selena standing outside watching a workman scale a telephone pole. His penetrating gaze lingered on her hair pulled into a ponytail before it traveled downward to a white camp shirt she'd tucked into the waistband of a pair of skinny jeans. The outline of her breasts under the shirt and the roundness of her hips quietly shouted her obvious femininity.

He slowed his approach, studying her delicate profile as she tilted her chin to watch the man perched atop the pole. Xavier didn't know what it was about Selena Yates, but there was something special about her. Xavier was less than a few feet from Selena when she turned and stared at him. Her expression of uncertainty gave way to recognition as her lips parted in a smile.

"Hello again, Xavier," she said in greeting.

His eyebrows lifted. "So, you remembered my name."

Selena's smile grew wider. She wanted to tell Xavier Eaton that not only had she remembered his name but also his gorgeous face and magnificent body. The man was the walking, breathing personification of everything exquisite about the male species.

"I remember all of my regular customers."

He took a few steps bringing them only inches apart. She had to tilt her head to meet his eyes. "What makes you think I'm going to be a regular customer?"

"Don't play yourself, Mr. Eaton. You're here two days in a row."

Xavier felt his pulse quicken when she lowered her seductive voice. "Yes."

Selena forced herself not to look below his neck. Today he'd worn a long-sleeved pale blue shirt with a pair of black tailored slacks. She'd noticed with his approach the corps insignia on the buckle on his black leather belt. It was apparent Xavier Eaton was a marine in every sense of the word. It was as if he'd taken the service motto, Once a Marine Always a Marine, quite seriously.

"Did your mother and sister like their gifts?"

Xavier nodded again. "That's why I'm here. They both loved them. My sister tried calling you to place an order, but got a busy signal."

Selena pointed to the man on the pole. "That's why they're here. My phone has been out all day. I can't call out or receive incoming calls. Of course, the disruption also affects my internet service."

"Can't you access the internet on your cell?"

"No! Once I leave the shop I try and distance myself from business, if only for a few hours. Having internet access on my cell is a temptation I'm not willing to risk."

"Are you still taking orders?"

"Sure. Please come inside."

Xavier found himself watching the gentle sway of Selena's hips as she turned and walked into the shop. She hadn't worn a hint of makeup, and he found her natural beauty refreshing. He wasn't into women who wore fake hair, nails and eyelashes because he didn't know whether he could touch them or not.

He'd dated one woman who wore makeup to bed, and even after several washings the stains from the makeup were still visible on the pillowcase and sheets. Another wouldn't let him touch her hair, and another one didn't want him to touch her breasts. To say that those relationships ended before they began was putting it mildly. All of the women were intelligent and attractive, but they'd come with a boatload of issues. When he shared a bed with a woman, nothing was off-limits.

Selena stared over her shoulder at Xavier as he glanced around the patisserie. Her last customer had left fifteen minutes ago, and in another hour she would close the shop. She doubted whether she would get too many more customers with the street blocked off to traffic. She would've closed earlier, but she was waiting for someone to pick up an order for a restaurant.

"What time do you close?" Xavier asked.

Her smile was dazzling. He'd read her mind. "Normally at six, but with no phone and the street closed to traffic I'm going to close early. I'm waiting for a pickup and then I'm out of here."

Xavier walked over to the table with the shipping slips, and retrieved his BlackBerry. He jotted down the Brandywine Valley address of the Tuckers in the delivery section. "I'd like to order a brownie-fudge cheesecake and a pound of chocolate-and-peanut-butter pretzels."

"When do you need them and where are they being shipped to?"

Selena stared at Xavier; he met her curious gaze with a penetrating one of his own. It had been a long time since she'd found a man intriguing and was uncertain why she felt strangely connected to him. Maybe it had something to do with his being in the military service. She wasn't superficial, so her attraction to him wasn't simply because of his handsome appearance. That was something she'd done as a teenager. At twenty-six she wanted to believe she was beyond the goo-goo-eyes stage in the presence of an attractive man. Yet the man standing in her shop, Xavier Eaton, had proven her wrong.

"They're to be shipped to . . ." Xavier's

words trailed off when the bell above the door chimed. He stood straighter, his eyes widening in surprise. "Bell?"

The tall dark-skinned man with a shaved pate, mustache and goatee stopped short. "Holy . . ." He swallowed the expletive at the last possible moment. "Eaton?"

Xavier took a step, finding himself in a bear hug that nearly crushed his ribs, and making it difficult for him to breathe. He pounded the broad back of the man he hadn't seen since they'd graduated from The Citadel. He rarely read the alumna updates online and had lost contact with many of his former classmates.

Robert Bell pulled back, released Xavier and shook his head. "What the hell are you doing in Charleston? Wait, don't tell me. You're Selena's mystery man."

CHAPTER 3

Xavier stared at Bobby Bell as if he'd taken leave of his senses. What was he talking about? And why did Bobby believe he had a connection to Selena. Today was only the second time they'd been seen with each other. His gaze shifted to Selena, his instincts suddenly on alert. There was something in her eyes that wordlessly communicated not to say anything.

Selena breathed an inaudible sigh when Xavier clamped his jaw. "Did you think I really didn't have someone, Robert Bell?" she drawled sarcastically.

"Will someone please tell me what's going on?" Xavier asked.

Bobby crossed massive arms over a broad, deep chest. "I run a restaurant with my dad and uncles, and on Fridays we have date night with a live jazz combo. I've been asking Selena to come, but she says she doesn't go anywhere without her boyfriend. Whenever I ask about her 'boyfriend' she always says he's busy. So after a while I started calling him her mystery man."

Bobby told Xavier more about Selena Yates in less than sixty seconds than he would've learned if he'd continued to come to her patisserie a dozen more times. She was single, wasn't dating anyone and no doubt a very private person. He took several steps and put his arm around her waist.

"I hope you're not calling *my woman* a liar, Bobby."

"No, no, no, man," Bobby countered, holding up his hands defensively. "It's just that I didn't know you were back in Charleston, that's all. One of the guys from school told me about you saving three of your men after they'd driven over an IED and —"

"We'll talk about *that* later," Xavier interrupted when he felt Selena's back go rigid against his arm. He didn't know if Bobby knew that her brother had served, as well.

Bobby's boyish round face softened when he winked at Selena. It was apparent Xavier didn't want to talk about the war in front of her. "I'm going to have to pick up those trays and head back to the restaurant. The kid who usually does all the runs sprained his ankle playing football, so yours truly is standing in as temporary gofer. Am I going to see you two tonight?" he asked Selena.

Xavier stared at Selena, lifting his eyebrows questioningly. "I'll come, that is if Selena isn't busy." He felt conflicting emotions. On the one hand he had hoped she'd be busy, since he'd never liked being manipulated into situations. But on the other hand, he'd hoped she wasn't busy, and going out with her would satisfy his curiosity.

Selena felt the powerful arm around her waist. She also enjoyed the way Xavier's body pressed against hers and the tantalizing scent of his cologne. She'd tired of Bobby Bell asking her to come to his family's restaurant for date night, because there wasn't any man she'd seen or met since moving to Charleston that she'd wanted to accompany her. It wasn't that men hadn't asked her out. But her involvement with a man who'd threatened her life if he couldn't have her, made her overly cautious when it came to dating. However, there was something about Xavier Eaton that reminded her of her brothers, and there was never a time when they hadn't protected her.

The boys in her West Virginia town knew if they messed with Selena Yates then they had to not only deal with her father but also her brothers. If their father hadn't been sheriff, there was little doubt either one or both would've spent several nights in the local jail. They'd protected her at home, but they were unable to protect her once she'd moved away.

"What about it, Selena? Do you want to go?" Xavier said when she gave Bobby a blank stare.

"Yes," she replied as if coming out of a trance. Her eyelids fluttered wildly when she realized what she'd agreed to.

Bobby's head bobbed up and down. "Good." He slapped Xavier's shoulder. "Mama is going to lose it when she sees you."

Xavier smiled. "Let your mother know that I'm looking forward to seeing her again."

Selena plastered on a smile. "Bobby, your order is in the back." She waited until Bobby made his way to the rear of the shop before rounding on Xavier. "Don't you dare say anything until after he leaves," she whispered.

Narrowing his eyes, Xavier pushed his face close to Selena's. "You have a lot of explaining to do, Ms. Yates."

Bobby emerged from the back, clutching four white shopping bags with *Sweet Persuasions* and the street address stamped on the sides. "Try to get there before seven, because Ma Bell's gets real crowded around eight."

"You named the restaurant Ma Bell's?"

Bobby laughed, the sound coming from deep within his wide chest. "Ma is short for Emma. We were going to call it Bell's, but my dad overruled his brothers. He said if his wife was going to cook alongside them, then the place would also bear her name. She cooks on Fridays and Saturdays, while they take over the kitchen from Sunday through Thursday."

Xavier nodded. "Good choice." He'd lost track of the number of times he'd sat at Emma Bell's table devouring everything she'd put in front of him. She was one of the best, if not *the* best, cook in the low country. He took his arm from around Selena, and opened the door for Bobby. "We'll see you later." He closed and locked the door, turned over the sign to Closed in the shop window, then turned to face Selena. "Please tell me why Bobby thinks I'm your mystery man?"

Selena closed her eyes for several seconds. "You don't have to go with me if you don't want to."

He closed the distance between them, grasped her shoulders and steered her over to one of the bistro tables. He pulled out a chair for her, then rounded the small table and sat on the opposite side. "If there is one thing you should know about me, Selena, it's that I'm not into playing head games. You tell Bobby you're going with me, and now you say I don't have to go. What's it going to be?"

Selena's hands tightened into fists, her nails biting into the tender flesh on her palms. She welcomed the pain rather than stare at the man glaring at her. "It's complicated, Xavier."

"How complicated can it be?" he countered. "Apparently you lied to Bobby about having a boyfriend, or do you really have a boyfriend stashed away somewhere?"

Her gaze swung back to his handsome face. "I don't have a boyfriend."

Xavier leaned over the table. "You don't have a boyfriend, yet you told Bobby you did. Why?"

She breathed an audible sigh. "I got tired of him asking me to come to Ma Bell's for date night, because he said if I didn't have someone to go with then he would hook me up with someone." Her delicate jaw tightened. "The last time someone hooked me up with a man it ended in disaster." What she didn't tell Xavier was that the relationship had almost cost her her life.

"I don't like being set up, either," Xavier said. "How long did you think you'd be able to string Bobby along without him becoming suspicious?"

Xavier's query elicited a smile from Selena. "It worked, didn't it?"

"It did until I became your date."

"You didn't have to go along with it."

A hint of a smile tilted the corners of his mouth upward. "But I did because I was curious to see how it would all play out. Now that I have a girlfriend I didn't know I had when I woke up this morning, perhaps you can tell me a little about yourself."

Selena felt the invisible wall she'd put up whenever she discovered a man getting too close to her emotionally disappear. "There's not much to tell."

Propping his elbow on the table, Xavier rested his chin on the heel of his hand. "Let me be the judge of that."

"Why are you going along with this, Xavier? I'm certain you'd rather take some other woman with you to Ma Bell's."

His impassive expression did not change. "Perhaps you weren't listening when I told you that I didn't have a girlfriend — that is until a few minutes ago. Now, baby, please tell me what I need to know about you so we can put on a winning performance for my old college buddy."

Selena didn't want to believe he'd called her "baby." The endearment rolled off his tongue like watered silk. "I'm twenty-six."

"When will you be twenty-seven?"

"October eighteenth."

"Are you a native Charlestonian?"

Selena shook her head. "No. I'm originally from West Virginia."

"Where in West Virginia?" he asked. Xavier had detected a slight accent, but he hadn't been able to identify where she was from.

"Matewan."

Lowering his arm, he stared at Selena as a shiver of excitement rushed over him. "I've never been to Matewan, although it has been on my list of must-see places."

"There isn't a whole lot to see," Selena replied. "It's a speck on the map."

"It's speck with a lot of history. Isn't it referred to as 'a peaceful place with a violent history'?"

Selena sat up straight. "How'd you know that?"

"I teach American history."

"Where?"

"At the Christopher Munroe Military Academy in North Charleston."

"Do you like teaching?" she asked, continuing with her questioning.

Xavier smiled, bringing her gaze to linger on his sexy mouth. "I love it. Now, tell me why you left Matewan."

"I was offered a full academic scholarship to Stanford."

The seconds ticked as he stared at Selena. Not only was his pretend girlfriend beautiful, but she was also very bright. "What was your major?"

"Drama."

"You're an actress?"

Slumping in the chair, Selena stared at a spot over Xavier's shoulder. Answering his question would open a door to her past she didn't want to reopen. "No," she half lied after a pronounced pause. "I'm a pastry chef."

"But . . . but why did you major in drama if you wanted to be a pastry chef?"

"At the time I didn't know that acting wasn't for me."

What she didn't tell Xavier was that she was a pastry chef with chocolate as her specialty. She prayed Xavier hadn't watched daytime soap operas or he would've recognized her even without the makeup and designer clothes. After she'd graduated, she'd auditioned for a small part on a soap opera and was hired on the spot. Her acting credits included commercials, a made-for-television movie and work in several films. The seven-episode role on the soap opera was expanded, and she was signed to a one-year contract and became a recurring character.

Ratings for the show escalated. Her workdays began at five in the morning and didn't end until ten at night. After memorizing fifty to sixty-page scripts, she barely had time for socializing. But after about a year and a half she began going out with Derrick Perry.

He'd been the most attentive man she'd ever known, but when his attentiveness bordered on obsession, Selena knew they had to stop seeing so much of each other. It was as if she were being smothered. He'd become unreasonable when she'd told him that she wasn't able to see him every day, and that they could get together on weekends. He'd fly into a rage, and then resort to a crying jag. She didn't see Derrick for several weeks, and when he reappeared it was as if nothing had happened. Selena didn't ask where he'd been and he hadn't been forthcoming about his disappearance. They'd resumed their weekends-only dating for a month when he disappeared again. This time it was for three months. When he'd shown up at her apartment late one Sunday night she didn't recognize the man with whom she'd been involved. He'd lost weight, his eyes were sunken, he'd grown a beard and his hair was fashioned into twists. When she'd asked where he'd been, his response was he'd gone away to try and find himself. It was then that he began stalking her and unbeknownst to her, planning to kill her.

"Selena?"

Xavier's voice broke into her thoughts. "Yes?"

"How often do you do that?"

"Do what?" she asked.

"Zone out."

Droplets of heat pricked her face. "I'm sorry. What else do you need to know about me?"

"How long have you lived in Charleston?"

"About a year and a half. I opened Sweet Persuasions six months ago. I've never been married and you already know I'm not involved with anyone."

"Is that by choice?"

A soft gasp escaped Selena's lips. She sat there stunned, unable to believe Xavier had asked her that question. "Of course it's by choice."

"Don't act so put out, Ms. Yates. After all, you were the one who said you didn't like people hooking you up. Suppose you'd met someone you liked. Would you get involved?"

Resting her elbows on the table, she shortened the small distance separating them. "Are you asking if I would consider seeing you, Mr. Eaton?" There was a hint of laughter in her voice.

Xavier eyes lingered on her parted lips before meeting her amused gaze. "No. I would never be that presumptuous," he said, unaware that his approval rating had gone up several points with Selena.

She wrinkled her nose. "Now it's your turn. Give me a quick overview of Xavier Eaton so I don't embarrass myself when someone asks me about my date."

"I'm thirty-four, a marine —"

"I thought you were no longer active military."

He wagged his finger. "Shame on you. Didn't your brother teach you, Once a Marine Always a Marine?"

"Now, how could I forget that?" Selena said jokingly, as she hit her forehead.

"I don't know," Xavier crooned.

She rolled her eyes at him. "I owe you for that one." Xavier responded with a wink. Suddenly he appeared carefree and boyish, qualities she didn't think he possessed.

Xavier curbed the urge to run his finger

down the length of Selena's nose. He didn't know what it was about her utterly adorable nose that captivated him. "I met Bobby Bell when we were cadets at The Citadel. I lived on campus while Bobby commuted. When I didn't go home to Philadelphia for holidays and school breaks, I could be found at Bobby's house. I became his unofficial brother. We managed to stay in touch after graduation, but lost contact with each other once he was assigned to the American embassy in Istanbul. After I was deployed to Iraq, and later Afghanistan, I lost touch with everyone I knew at The Citadel."

The seconds ticked as Selena gave Xavier a long, penetrating stare. "Were you injured in combat?" He nodded, then went completely still as if he'd been carved out of stone. "Why did you decide to return to Charleston?" she asked, changing the topic.

Xavier breathed an audible sigh. He didn't like talking about the war because the images of what he'd done and seen were indelibly imprinted in his mind. There were times when he woke up struggling to breathe, his heart racing uncontrollably from the nightmares that haunted him once he was no longer on active duty.

"I like this city."

"You like this city?" Selena said.

"Isn't that enough?" Xavier said. "You moved from West Virginia to California to go to school, but instead of returning home you decided to put down roots in South Carolina."

"There's a reason why I didn't go back to West Virginia." She knew she sounded defensive, but Selena wasn't about to spill her guts to a man who she was just pretending to date.

Xavier crossed his injured right leg over his left knee. He was able to get around without a cane now, but there were times when the dull ache was a reminder of how close he'd come to losing the limb. "Were you running away from an old boyfriend?"

Years of acting training kicked in when Selena's face belied the tension of the knot that had formed in her stomach. She didn't and couldn't tell Xavier how close he was to the truth. "I didn't have a boyfriend when I lived in Matewan."

"Did you have one when you lived in California?"

"I thought we were talking about you?" she retorted, unable to hide her annoyance.

Folding his arms across his chest, Xavier angled his head and studied the woman who'd become more of an enigma with each passing minute. Initially she was open and friendly, willing to talk about anything. But, whenever he mentioned her involvement with a man she always managed to change the subject. He wondered if she'd had a bad relationship. She was an attractive, intelligent and talented twenty-six-year-old who probably had a steady stream of men coming into Sweet Persuasions just to catch a glimpse of her. Most women would revel in the attention, but for Selena it seemed to be just the opposite.

"I'm sorry if I hit a nerve."

"You didn't hit a nerve, Xavier. You were prying. After all, I didn't ask you about the women in your life."

A hint of a smile softened his mouth. "There are only two women in my life at the moment — my mother and sister."

It was Selena's turn to smile. "Is that your way of telling me that you're not involved with anyone?"

"I thought I was being subtle."

Her smile became a full-on grin. "I don't think so."

"Damn!" he drawled. "Is there anything else you need to know about me?"

"No."

There was a lot more Selena *wanted* to know about Xavier Eaton, but only if she'd been interested in becoming involved with him.

Xavier stood up. Their cross-examination had ended. He believed he'd garnered enough information about Selena to feel comfortable pretending to be her boyfriend. "I'd better give you that mailing information for the cheesecake and pretzels. When do you think they'll be shipped out?"

"That depends on if you want them delivered Sunday or Monday."

"I'd like a Sunday delivery." He completed the shipping form, handing it to Selena, who'd stood up. "How long will it take to get to Ma Bell's from here?"

"It shouldn't take more than ten minutes." Selena gave him the address.

Xavier didn't tell her the restaurant was less than a quarter mile from his house. Although he'd moved back to Charleston, he hadn't had the time to get acquainted with his adopted city. After he'd received his appointment to Munroe, he'd purchased a house in Charleston's historic district that needed extensive renovations. Before he relocated however, he used to drive from Philadelphia to Charleston every two weeks to look at the progress and confer with the contractor.

It wasn't until the first week of August

that he moved into his house, which was known as a Charleston single house. It was representative of the city's nineteenth-century period architecture, in which many houses were one-room wide for cross-ventilation, with each room opening into the next, fronting the street, with a full-length veranda on the side, often with a two-story porch overlooking a garden. Many of the rooms in Xavier's house were empty. Some were awaiting delivery of furniture, while others would remain empty until he decided how he wanted to decorate them. As long as he had something to sit on, eat on and a place to sleep, Xavier didn't feel the need to fill up his first home with things that didn't fit in.

"If I pick you up at six-thirty, will that give you enough time to get ready?"

Selena glanced at the wall clock. It was minutes after five. That meant she had a little more than an hour to get ready for her date. "It's enough time."

Reaching into the pocket of his slacks, Xavier removed his credit card. "Where shall I pick you up?"

"I'll meet you on the block behind the shop. I live upstairs," she explained when seeing his puzzled expression.

"Now that's what I call a sweet setup. You

never have to worry about the weather or getting tied up in traffic to get to work."

"It's nice. Sometimes when I can't sleep, I come down and bake." Selena waved away the card. "You're going to have to pay me later, after they restore telephone service."

Xavier returned the card to the case. "Are you always this trusting?"

"Don't play yourself, Xavier P. Eaton. Remember I have your credit card information on file. And if you try to stiff me, I'll bill your account for three times the amount."

"You wouldn't," he deadpanned.

"Oh, yes, I would. Remember, I come from coal-mining stock. There aren't too many folks tougher or more resilient than coal miners."

"One of these days I'd like to hear about it."

Selena shook her head. "I don't think that's going to happen, Xavier."

"Why, Selena?" His voice sounded low and seductive.

"That would mean another date."

He took a step, bringing them less than a foot apart. Everything that was Selena Yates swept over him, pulling him in and refusing to let him go. He'd tried to remain unaffected but he'd failed miserably. Somehow fate had stepped in when Robert Bell walked into Sweet Persuasions to find him with the owner of the patisserie. If his friend had assumed he and Selena were a couple, then he had no intention of correcting the mistake — especially not when he was given the opportunity to take her to dinner without having to work up the nerve to ask her out on a date. It wasn't his style to come on heavy with a woman, and it usually took several encounters before he would make his move. But Selena was different — just how different he had yet to discover.

"Would that be so horrible?"

Putting her hands on his rock-solid chest, Selena tried to put some space between them. She felt the warmth of his body through the fabric of his shirt. "No, it wouldn't, but why don't we just wait and see if we can tolerate each other enough to go out again."

Grabbing her wrists, Xavier held her captive. "Don't you think *tolerate* is too strong a word?"

Lowering her eyes, Selena peered up at him through her lashes. "I can't count the number of times I'm forced to *tolerate* dealing with someone — and that includes some of my customers."

"Is yours truly included in that group?"

"You will if you don't let me close up and get ready for my date night."

"I hear you loud and clear, Ms. Yates." Xavier released her wrists, lowered his head, brushing his mouth over hers in a kiss that was so light she thought she'd imagined it. "I'll see you later."

Selena barely had time to react before she registered the chiming of the bell that signaled Xavier had unlocked the door and left. On unsteady legs, she walked over to the door and locked it behind him.

She didn't know how it had happened, but within the span of half an hour she'd agreed to go to Ma Bell's for date night with a stranger — a handsome stranger, nonetheless — who until a few days ago she didn't even know existed. Pressing her back to the door, Selena closed her eyes. What, she mused, was there about Xavier Eaton that made her do and feel things that were totally out of character for practical, level-headed Selena Liliana Yates?

Grandma Lily had called her a hummingbird, forever in motion and her mind flitting from one thing to the other. When her grandfather, who was a carpenter, built her the grandest dollhouse she had ever seen, she'd announced she was going to decorate the rooms using scraps of leftover fabric from her grandmother's quilting and needlecraft projects. Hand-sewn curtains, crocheted rugs and wallpaper made from colorful adhesive-backed drawer liners were the envy of the girls who came to see what Selena had been bragging about. It had taken years for her to furnish the dollhouse with carefully chosen wood-looking tables and chairs, and appliances made from scrap metal. By the time she'd celebrated her fifteenth birthday she'd lost interest in decorating when she appeared on stage in a school play. The acting bug had bitten her — hard. The dollhouse, which was put in a room where her parents stored old cradles, cribs and other pieces of furniture made by her grandfather and great-grandfather, had been relegated to her childhood.

Never in her wildest dreams could Selena have predicted that she would walk away from acting. She'd barely tasted success when her world fell apart because a man who'd professed his love to her tried to hurt her. She shook her head as if to shake off the memory of Derrick. Working quickly, she transferred trays from the showcase to the walk-in freezer, turned off the lights, punched in the code to the alarm and locked the door behind her.

Selena unlocked the rear door to the staircase that led up to her apartment. Monica had picked up Trisha from school and driven up to Goose Creek to spend the weekend with her parents. Since her neighbor wasn't around she avoided having to explain why she was going out on a Friday night. As she opened the door to her apartment, she felt a flutter of excitement in the pit of her stomach much like she'd experienced when she had a crush on a boy who was her brother's friend. Each time he came to the house she scurried away like a frightened mouse, spending the entire time in her bedroom while she'd fantasized about kissing him. It was only when he began dating a girl Selena disliked intensely, that she decided not only was he ugly but he also had ears that stuck out too far.

But there was nothing wrong with Xavier Eaton — at least not on the surface. She had to be careful — very, very careful to look for the signs that he wasn't what he seemed to be. After what she'd experienced with Derrick, Selena had sworn it would never happen again.

Chapter 4

Xavier maneuvered up to the curb at the same time the door to the rear of the two-story building opened and one sling-back-shod foot touched the pavement, then another. As he stared out the windshield, he saw Selena glance to her right, then her left. Shifting into Park, he got out of his sports car and walked over to her.

A black pencil skirt that brushed her knees, a matching long-sleeved top that hugged her upper body like a second skin and four-inch heels had transformed Selena Yates into a sensual, sophisticated woman. A narrow silver belt around her slender waist and silver hoops in her lobes accented the all-black ensemble. Seeing the soft swell of breasts against the fitted top and the sexy curves of her hips in the slender skirt made it difficult for Xavier to control the heat racing through his veins. He couldn't remember the last time his body had betrayed him just by looking at a woman.

Her hair was pinned at the nape of her neck in a fashionable chignon. Without warning she turned, her raspberry-colored lips parting in a smile when she recognized him, while his gaze lingered on the smoky shadows of her eyelids. She was stunning!

Wrapping an arm around her waist, Xavier pressed his mouth to her ear. “You look amazing.”

Shifting her small evening clutch to the opposite hand, Selena rested her palm against the crisp fabric of Xavier’s white shirt. “Thank you.”

He’d changed his blue shirt for one with French cuffs, and had added an aubergine silk tie. The charcoal-gray slacks graced his tall physique as if they had been tailored expressly for him. She’d wanted to tell him he looked good enough to eat, but the compliment would probably make him think she was nothing more than a desperate, sex-starved woman, who had denied her libido for far too long. What he didn’t know and she hoped he would never know was how true it was. Even in stilettos, Xavier eclipsed her by at least two inches.

Xavier reached for her hand, gently squeezing her fingers. “Are you ready?”

Her smile spoke volumes. “Yes.”

She was ready for a night at Ma Bell's and she was ready for Xavier Eaton. She'd given herself a pep talk. For the first time in years she could afford to let her guard down for a few hours. Although she only knew what Xavier had told her about himself, an inner voice told her that she could trust him not to hurt her. He was a teacher after all, and had probably gone through an extensive background check. He had been in the military and had risked his own life to save others. She knew instinctively that it wasn't modesty that made him preempt Bobby Bell from recounting a war story, but that the memory of what he'd experienced was still too new and too traumatic to talk about now.

Xavier led her over to a gleaming, silver, late-model Porsche. He opened the passenger-side door, waiting until she was comfortably settled in the black-leather seat. "Your car has a new-car smell," Selena remarked when he folded his long frame behind the wheel.

Xavier pressed the button to start the engine, and the sports car roared to life as the engine purred. "It is."

"How long have you had it?"

"Five months."

Her gaze went to the dashboard of the 911

Carrera. "You must do a lot of driving." He had logged almost ten thousand miles on a car he'd had less than six months.

Resting his right arm over the back of her seat, Xavier ran a finger over the hair pinned on her neck. "I did a lot of driving between Philly and Charleston renovating my house. The first thought I had when I saw the house was to douse it in a flammable liquid and then drop a match."

Selena shifted in her seat as far as her seatbelt would allow as her gaze met and fused with Xavier's. "Why did you buy it?"

"The real estate agent said it had a lot of potential."

"Did it?"

Xavier smiled, attractive lines fanning out around his eyes. "It does now," he said cryptically.

Her eyes narrowed. "What did you do?"

"I undertook an extensive renovation."

"You're kidding?"

He shook his head. "No, I'm not. I wouldn't have bought it if it wasn't structurally sound, so I had an architect reconfigure the rooms and update the electrical and heating systems. The overall historical integrity of it is still intact. It's a Charleston single house, but the interior is definitely twenty-first century."

"Are the furnishings contemporary?"

Signaling, Xavier maneuvered away from the curb and into traffic. "I'm not certain."

Selena stared at his distinctive profile. "What aren't you certain about?"

Xavier gave his passenger a quick glance. "I've thought about hiring an interior decorator, but I don't want my home to look like a museum or like it's ready for a glossy magazine layout. Take your shop."

"What about my shop, Xavier?"

"Sweet Persuasions looks exactly like what it's supposed to be — a Parisian patisserie. And I want my home to reflect its architectural heritage — a Charleston single house. It doesn't matter whether the furnishings are eighteenth century or twenty-first century. I want it to look lived in."

"Have you thought of furnishing it with pieces from different periods so that it has an eclectic style?"

He came to a stop at a red light, staring out the windshield at the half dozen college students ambling across the street. Not an unusual sight for a city with at least eight colleges and universities, including an art institute and a medical school. On weekends, locals and tourists were forced to compete with students for space in the crowded clubs and restaurants.

"Talk to me, Selena Yates."

"Do your bedrooms having seating areas?"

"Yes. Why?"

"You can decorate the seating areas in an earlier time period, while the bedroom itself can reflect a more contemporary look."

The light changed and Xavier took off in a burst of speed. "Would you be willing to come by when you have some free time and look at my place?"

Selena turned her head, looking out the side window. Xavier wasn't talking about her seeing his place after they left Ma Bell's, but some other time. And to her that meant another encounter with Xavier Eaton. It was something she didn't know whether she was willing to risk because what she was beginning to feel for him defied description.

The moment the bell over the door at Sweet Persuasions rang and she'd looked up to see who had come into the patisserie, her reaction to seeing Xavier Eaton was one that was so completely foreign that even after he'd left she wondered whether she'd conjured him up. If she hadn't had his return address and credit card information she would've thought he was a figment of her very active imagination.

Yes, he was eye candy and also a lot more. And the "more" translated into intelligence and sophistication — something that was missing in a lot of men she'd met. *Tolerate* him. Selena couldn't believe the word had come out of her mouth. Ten minutes into their "date" and she couldn't imagine wanting to be anyplace other than in a sports car with a man who made her believe she *could* have a normal relationship.

"Sweet Persuasions is closed on Sunday and Monday, so it would have to be either of those days."

"What about Sunday?" Xavier asked. Both he and Selena were off on that day. "I'll prepare Sunday dinner for you."

She gave him an incredulous look. "You cook?"

"Did I stutter?" he quipped.

Selena wrinkled her nose. "When did you become a comedian?"

"Yes, darling, I cook."

"You don't have to call me darling when we're alone."

Xavier turned down the street leading to Ma Bell's. "I was just rehearsing. After all, you're the actress."

"Former actress," Selena said, correcting him.

Xavier scanned both sides of the cobblestone street for a parking space. "Once an actor, always an actor. I'm willing to bet you can change the sound of your voice without having to think about it. Well, can you?" he asked when he was met with silence.

Xavier's questions about her acting career had aroused old fears Selena thought she'd buried when she left Los Angeles.

"Would you mind if we don't discuss my past?"

"It's your call, Selena. If you don't want to talk about your past, then we won't."

Selena noted the edge in his voice. "There's no need to get snippy about it, Xavier."

He rolled his eyes at her. "FYI — I don't get snippy. I get annoyed and at times angry, but I never get snippy. Women get snippy."

"Ohhh! Don't tell me I'm dating a sexist."

Xavier found a space between a Hummer and a Navigator, deftly maneuvering until there was enough room between the front and rear bumpers of the oversize vehicles. He cut off the engine, released his seatbelt and then turned to face the woman inches from him. Light coming through the windshield cast long and short shadows over her beautiful face. His eyes moved over her features like the whisper of a caress.

"I may be many things, but there is one thing I'm not. And that is sexist. I like women, Selena. All types of women," he added, his voice sounding lower until it was barely a whisper. "And it doesn't matter whether they're light, dark, slim or full-figured. I've done a great deal of traveling and that means I've met a lot of women. Some I've dated and some were there when I needed someone to talk to, and I've never abused a woman physically or emotionally."

"You've dated out of your race?" Selena asked, staring at his mouth.

A smile softened Xavier's firm mouth. "Out of my race, religion and ethnic group," he confirmed. "The only prerequisite is she be comfortable with who she is." Leaning to his right, Xavier pressed his mouth to her moist, parted lips. "Do it again, Daddy," he said in a high-pitched voice.

Selena laughed until tears filled her eyes, unaware that Xavier was staring at her as if she'd suddenly taken leave of her senses. "You are hilarious," she said, dabbing the corners of her eyes with her forefinger.

His expressive eyebrows lifted questioningly. "Why am I hilarious, Selena?"

She sobered. "You're funny when you imitate a woman." Selena rested her hand on his clean-shaven jaw. "Is that what they call you?"

He nodded, winking. "Sometimes it's Big

Daddy."

"Well, damn, Xavier Eaton. It's like that?"

"So they say."

They smiled at each other. "Have you no shame?" Selena asked.

Xavier's smile grew wider. "No."

The single word was uttered so innocently that Selena laughed again. She knew very little about him, but something told her hanging out with him was going to be a lot of fun. She leaned into him, brushing a light kiss over his mouth. "Let's go, Big Daddy. There's a line forming outside Ma Bell's, and I don't want to have to stand waiting in these heels."

"You don't have to worry about your feet hurting, sweetheart. I'll carry you."

"Thanks, but no thanks, Daddy," she crooned, her voice becoming a sensual purr.

Xavier felt the flesh between his thighs stir to life, as he swallowed a groan of frustration. His body had betrayed him for the second time that night. What, he mused, was there about Selena Yates that had him lusting after her like a horny adolescent boy? It had been a long time — a very long time since he hadn't been in control of his sexual urges. There were periods when he'd gone without a woman, yet he'd been able to quell those urges. But, it was different with

Selena. He doubted ice-cold showers would be enough.

"You're right. Let's get in line before we have to wait for a table."

Opening the driver's side door, he stepped out, reached for his suit jacket, slipped his arms into the sleeves and went around the car to help Selena. Xavier forced himself not to stare at her long, smooth, bare brown legs in the sexy heels. When his sister had asked what made a woman special he hadn't been able to explain it to her. However, if she'd asked again, then he would be able to tell her. Selena Yates was special — very special.

Cradling her hand in the bend of his arm, he led her down the street to Ma Bell's. Those on line were casual, chic, twenty- and thirtysomething couples. The men were attentive to their dates, gazing adoringly into their eyes, or had angled their heads to hear what their women were saying. He overheard the couple in front of him talk about how much they'd enjoyed date night at Ma Bell's and were looking forward to doing it again. Their declaration echoed what Xavier felt at that moment. If this date night proved positive, then he hoped there would be many more with Selena.

■ ■ ■ ■

Selena didn't know what to expect when she and Xavier were finally directed inside the restaurant, but it wasn't the nightclub decor and ambiance. Tables and chairs were replaced with booths and banquettes with seating for two, four, six or eight. Dim recessed lighting and flickering votives on each table made it the perfect setting for seduction and romance. The brightest illumination came from the stage where a quintet was warming up.

Bobby, who'd greeted them warmly, appeared less imposing dressed in all black. He and Xavier exchanged greetings. "We've got a full house tonight, so I hope you don't mind if I pair you with another couple at a table for four."

Xavier frowned. He'd hoped he wouldn't have to share Selena with anyone else. This was their first date and he wanted it to be just them. He gave her hand a gentle squeeze. "What's the alternative, Bobby?"

"You'll have to wait for a free table for two, and that may take hours. Look, man, the couple you'll be seated with are okay. If not, then everything is on the house."

He wanted to tell his former classmate

that it wasn't about money, but about wanting to be alone with his pretend girlfriend so she could possibly become a *real* girlfriend.

Leaning into her, Xavier inhaled the subtle scent of her sensual perfume. "It's up to you, baby. Do you mind sharing a table with another couple?"

Selena patted Xavier's hard shoulder over his suit jacket. "Of course I don't mind," she said much too quickly, and resisted the urge to laugh out loud.

Sharing a table with another couple would cool things down between her and Xavier. It would also give her the chance to observe him in a social setting. *If* she did agree to go out with Xavier again, then she would make certain to take it slowly — very, very slowly.

"Good," Bobby whispered under his breath. "Please follow me."

It had been some time since Selena had put on a pair of stilettos, and navigating the dimly lit restaurant without turning an ankle would end in success or embarrassing failure. Hopefully it would be the former rather than latter. Miraculously Xavier must have been reading her mind because he shortened his stride to match hers.

Bobby slapped Xavier on his shoulder. "Brother, I believe you're familiar with the gentleman. But, in case you've forgotten — Major Eaton, I'd like to reintroduce you to First Lieutenant Douglas Mayer, USMC."

A tall, slender, deeply tanned man, with cropped sandy-brown hair stood up, coming to attention and saluting Xavier before the two men enveloped each other in a bear hug. "How the hell have you been?" Xavier asked, grinning at the lieutenant who'd rounded out the trio when they were cadets at The Citadel.

"It's been nothing but good," Douglas said, his wide grin matching Xavier's.

As if on cue, Xavier, Douglas and Bobby draped their arms around one another's shoulders and shouted, "Ooh-rah!" Those in Ma Bell's recognized the marine corps battle cry and echoed them. There were even a few female voices among them.

Selena felt as if she were back in Matewan, because whenever Luke's buddies came to visit it was all about the corps. It was as if they breathed, ate and dreamed about the marine corps.

Bobby winked at Selena and then the woman in the booth with Douglas. "I'm going to have to get back to the door but you guys, and *ladies* enjoy. Someone will be over to take your food and beverage order."

Putting his hand around Selena's waist,

Xavier helped her to the booth, then sat down beside her, resting his hand at the small of her back. "Selena, I'd like you to meet Douglas Mayer. He, Bobby and I were referred to as the Unholy Triumvirate, because we graduated one, two and three in the class. Doug, Selena Yates."

Reaching across the table, Doug shook Selena's hand. The glow from the candle illuminated in his light brown eyes. Every strand on his head was precisely cut like a manicured lawn. "It's my pleasure, Selena. The beautiful woman sitting next to you is my wife, Leandra."

Selena smiled and nodded to the woman with spiral curls framing a face that matched the color and texture of milk chocolate. "It's nice meeting you, Leandra."

Leandra Mayer waved her hand. "Please call me Lee. And it's nice meeting you, Selena." She winked at Xavier across the table. "You haven't changed, X-man."

Xavier returned her wink with one of his own. He didn't want to believe that Douglas, who'd dated Leandra months before their graduation, had finally married his longtime girlfriend. He berated himself for not staying in contact with his friends. After his first tour of duty to Iraq he hadn't wanted to talk to anyone. After the second tour it was as if he'd become emotionally numb. He'd stopped reading the email updates about the cadets from his graduating class because they belonged to a time and place where things were different. War was neither safe nor very predictable.

"Neither have you, Lee."

She laughed. "You wouldn't say that if I stood up."

"Lee is six months pregnant with our first baby," Doug announced proudly.

Leaning over, Xavier slapped his friend's shoulder. "Congratulations! Would you mind if I order a bottle of champagne and sparkling cider for the mother-to-be?"

Leandra smiled at her husband before shifting her gaze to Xavier. "Thank you."

"You're carrying the baby very well," Selena said to Leandra. Although she hadn't stood up, she still wasn't able to discern that she was pregnant.

"It's the top. It conceals a lot," Leandra teased. "How long have you known Xavier?"

"Not long," she said.

Leandra folded her hands together on the white tablecloth, the diamonds on her left hand giving off blue and white sparks. "I always had a crush on him," she whispered, shooting furtive glances in Xavier's direction as he laughed at something her husband had said.

Selena moved closer to Leandra. "Did he know it?" she whispered like a coconspirator.

"No, and I never worked up the nerve to say anything. I was a student at the art institute and some of my friends would hang out at a spot where cadets from The Citadel gathered on the weekends. Doug, Bobby and Xavier were inseparable, and when Doug asked me to go to the movies with him I said yes because I thought Xavier would come along. Much to my chagrin it was just Doug and me and I later learned they never double- or triple-dated."

"But it worked out because you two are married."

Leandra rolled her eyes. "Please, girl, don't get me started about how long it took for us to finally make it to the altar."

Selena laughed. There was something about Leandra Mayer she liked. She was unpretentious, a quality that probably endeared her to her husband. "We'll talk about *our* men at another time," she said. Selena knew if Leandra told her about Douglas, then she'd want to know about her and Xavier. They had to get through at least one date for Selena to think of themselves as a couple. "Where do you go for your hair?" Whenever Leandra moved her head her curls moved as if they had a life of their own.

"I do my own hair."

"You're kidding?"

"No, I'm not," Leandra admitted. She flashed a smug smile. "My aunt owns a salon, and I used to help her. I'd sweep up, sort laundry and stock shelves. By the time I was thirteen I became her shampoo girl. Not only did I get tips from her clients, but Aunt Flora took me to the bank where she opened an account for my college fund, matching dollar for dollar everything I deposited. I'd learned to set and style hair. But she wouldn't let me, even though I knew how, to cut, dye and perm because I didn't have a license."

"How are you able to set the back of your head?" Selena asked.

"I use two mirrors. If you want I can do yours."

Selena shook her head. "No, that's all right."

"I don't mind, Selena. I'm not working, so I have more time than I know what to do with on my hands. I've knitted so many sweaters, booties and blankets that I could open a shop."

She wanted to tell her that if she did open

a shop, then she would complain that there weren't enough hours in the day to do everything she needed to do. Even when she wasn't working Selena was working — if only in her head. She was always thinking of new desserts and pastries. Chocolate truffles, amaretto truffle squares, nougat and croquant candies and nougat chocolates. But it was the cookies, tarts and cakes that taxed her imagination.

"I'll let you know," she told Leandra. It had taken her a while to find a salon. There had been times when she'd spent more time sitting and waiting for service than it took to wash, condition, set, dry and comb out her hair.

She jumped slightly when Xavier placed his hand on her knee. "Are you hungry?" he whispered in her ear.

"Yes." And she was. He opened the menu, as she pressed her shoulder to his to read the selections. Ma Bell's offered a variety of low-country cuisine.

"Do you see anything you like?"

Selena gave him a sidelong glance. "Yes. Everything looks good."

"If Emma Bell is doing the cooking, then everything is delicious."

"Did I just hear someone call my name?"

Xavier's head popped up seconds before

he came to his feet. Douglas also stood up. The woman who'd welcomed him into her home as if he were one of her sons stood in front of their table, hands at her waist over a bibbed apron. Wrapping his arms around her waist, he lifted her off her feet while kissing her cheek. "Mama Bell. You're as beautiful as ever."

Emma kissed her son's friend. "And you're a beautiful liar, Xavier Philip Eaton. Or should I say Major Eaton." She waved to Douglas. "Sit down, Doug."

Xavier set the tall, rawboned woman on her feet. It had been almost eight years since he'd last seen Emma. He'd come to Charleston to visit Bobby days after he'd received orders that he was to be deployed. Unfortunately, he and Bobby had missed each by several hours. His plane was touching down in Charleston, while Bobby was en route to Turkey.

It was as if time stood still. Her strong Gullah features hadn't changed and her dark brown skin was unlined, although she'd begun graying in her early thirties. "I'm no longer in the military."

Emma patted his chest. "It don't matter, son. You're a war hero. When Bobby told me you were coming by I decided to make something real special for you and Doug.

So don't bother looking at the menu." She smiled at Leandra. "I'll make certain you get something that's not too spicy. Can't have that baby giving you heartburn." Her gaze shifted to Selena. "Good evening, Selena. Your desserts are very popular at Ma Bell's."

She smiled. "Thank you, Ms. Emma."

"I'm going to need you to double our usual order, because we're starting to put them out for Sunday's gospel brunch."

Selena nodded. "I'll call you tomorrow."

"Call me before ten. It's nice that you and Xavier are keeping company."

She felt a wave of heat creep up her hairline. "Yes, ma'am."

Emma flashed a wide smile. "I'll have someone bring out your food." She gave Xavier another kiss. "How long are you going to be in Charleston?"

"Hopefully for a long time. I bought a house here and I'm also teaching in North Charleston."

"Does the owner of Sweet Persuasions have anything to do with you putting down roots here?" she said in his ear.

Xavier chuckled. "Maybe."

Taking his arm, Emma led him a short distance away from the table. "You better not mess over that girl the way Douglas did with Leandra. It was only when he thought he was going to lose her that he asked her to marry him."

"We haven't quite reached the stage where we're talking about marriage, Ms. Emma. And I've never messed over a woman."

"Good for you. I have to get back to the kitchen. I want you to come by the house with Selena. I'm only here on Friday and Saturday, so you will find me home all the other days."

"We'll come by," Xavier said, speaking for himself and Selena. He realized he was being presumptuous, and hoped Selena would agree to accompany him.

Reaching into the pocket of her apron, Emma pulled out a hairnet and covered her salt-and-pepper natural as she turned and walked back to the restaurant kitchen. Had he and Selena gotten themselves into a situation they wouldn't be able extricate themselves from? What if she decided after tonight that she didn't want to see him again? He'd always heard that when you tell one lie you had to tell another to cover that one. He prayed tonight's lie would be the last one he would have to concoct.

He dropped down beside Selena at the same time two waiters approached the table — one carrying an ice bucket with a bottle of champagne and the other balancing a tray filled with covered entrées on his shoulder. A third approached with a quartet of flutes and a chilled bottle of sparkling cider.

The waiter with the tray set it on a collapsible stand. "Everything is on the house tonight," he announced as he set out dishes and flatware before he uncovered dishes from which wafted delicious, mouthwatering smells.

Selena barely heard the soft popping sound of the champagne cork when it was removed from the bottle as she stared at the okra gumbo, pork chops with gravy, fried chicken, collard greens, fried crab rice, butter beans and oxtail with ham hocks. There was enough food on the table for at least ten people.

"I'm hungry, not starving," she said sotto voce.

Xavier dropped a kiss on her hair. "Doug and I can eat more than half of what is on this table, so I doubt if there will be any doggy bags."

"How do you stay so fit?"

"I try to log about two miles a day on a treadmill."

His orthopedist had recommended he either join a health club or purchase a treadmill and walk every day to strengthen the muscles in his right leg. He'd bought the exercise equipment, setting it up in a spare room with southern exposure. Within minutes of his feet touching the floor in the morning Xavier found himself on the treadmill, walking and watching an early morning news show on the wall-mounted television.

The sommelier filled three flutes with champagne and the remaining one with the nonalcoholic bubbling beverage. "Who gets the virgin bubbly?"

Leandra gestured. "I do."

Waiting until everyone was given a glass, Xavier raised his in a toast. "To Doug and Lee and baby makes three. Congratulations."

"Here, here," everyone chorused.

Douglas extended his flute. "To my brother from another mother — semper fi."

Smiling, Xavier nodded. "Semper fi."

Leandra swallowed a mouthful of cider. "If I didn't come from a family of military men I'd really say that my husband loves the corps more than me."

"You know I love you and our baby," Douglas crooned, tugging at a curl falling over Leandra's forehead.

Selena shared a smile with Xavier when he placed his hand on her thigh under the table. The gesture was natural, nonthreatening. She placed her hand on his, threading their fingers together. If tonight was any indication of what she could look forward to when going out with Xavier, then she was ready to jump back into the dating game.

"May I please have everyone's attention for a few minutes." Bobby Bell stood on the stage with a handheld microphone. The murmur of voices faded to a hushed silence, all gazes trained on the man standing under the circle of a spotlight. "Good evening ladies and gentlemen and welcome to Ma Bell's date night. For those who are here with someone they shouldn't be, this is the time to make your escape. Don't worry, management will dim the lights to protect your identity." Applause and unrestrained laughter followed his announcement. "Every date night is special, but tonight the Holy City would like to welcome home the final third of the Unholy Triumvirate. Friend, buddy and brother, Major Xavier Eaton, will you please stand up?"

Selena felt Xavier's hand tighten into a fist. "Get up," she whispered. He stood.

"Lieutenant Douglas Mayer, will you please stand up, too?" Adjusting his suit jacket, Douglas rose to his feet. "Everyone military, active or retired, please stand up."

Heads turned, when one by one men and women came to their feet. "Every date night at Ma Bell's is special, but tonight is even more so, because I'm dedicating it to Major Eaton. Despite being seriously injured, he risked his own life to save those of his men who were injured by an IED. Members of the waitstaff will give those of you standing a yellow ticket. Be certain to hand in the ticket when your server gives you the check, because tonight Ma Bell's will pick up your tab to thank you for your service and the sacrifices you've made for our country." Whistles, catcalls and shouts filled the restaurant. Bobby tapped the microphone. "Eat, drink, listen to good music and get home safe." He placed the microphone on its stand, bumping fists with members of the band.

Xavier sat, clenching his teeth in frustration. Bobby had thrust him into the spotlight, making him the poster boy for heroism. He'd returned to South Carolina to teach, not to become a local hero. He felt the gentle press and warmth of Selena's hand on his back.

Turning his head, he stared at her looking at him through her lashes. "Do you mind if I serve you?"

Her moist lips parted. "Of course not,"

she whispered, leaning in and pressing her mouth to his. "Congratulations, Major."

Xavier froze, then relaxed, deepening the kiss. He didn't know whether Selena had taken the initiative to kiss him because of his military record, or because it was what he'd wanted her to do. Each time he looked at her, touched her, it was as if he'd silently willed a response. It was with much reluctance that he pulled back, his eyes locked with hers until he was forced to look away. He, who never believed in displays of public affection, wanted to kiss Selena Yates — everywhere, and make love to her until he passed out from exhaustion.

Chapter 5

If asked, Selena would not have been able to explain why she'd kissed Xavier. Perhaps it had been her way of congratulating him for a selfless act of heroism, or maybe it was the champagne. After a few sips she felt free — freer than she had been in a very long time. The pressure of his firm mouth against hers, the taste and smell of his wine-scented breath mingling with his cologne and natural masculine scent had become a natural aphrodisiac that pulled her into a hypnotic spell of desire. The only thing she knew about Xavier Eaton was what he'd shown her, and what he'd revealed about himself and she wanted him!

Blinking as if she'd come out of a trance, Selena glanced around at those sitting in the booth. Everyone was staring at her as if she was expected to say something. Had she zoned out again? She shifted her gaze to the food on her plate, and picked up the fork at her place setting to eat what Xavier had served her. The sounds of live jazz, blues and R&B provided the perfect background for scrumptious food, good company and witty, engaging, intelligent conversation.

Leandra kept everyone entertained when she'd described the field trips she'd taken with her middle school art classes. Invariably one or two students would go beyond the barriers set up to keep patrons a safe distance from the works of art to personally examine a painting or statue.

"I'm embarrassed to say that after the second field trip my school got a letter from the museum stating that our students were banned from attending exhibits for three years."

Selena chewed and swallowed a forkful of tender collard greens. "They couldn't have been that bad."

Leandra shook her head. "These kids were definitely out of control. It wasn't until I'd announced that there would be no more field trips to the museum that they cheered, and then I realized they'd deliberately acted out."

"A couple of years at a military boot camp will straighten out any kid," Xavier remarked.

"I agree," Doug remarked. "I've already

told Lee that our son or daughter will have to salute me, and call me sir, not daddy."

"Yeah, right," Leandra drawled facetiously.

The expression on Selena's face spoke volumes. She couldn't believe a man would want his child to relate to him as if they were a stranger. "Are you serious?" she asked when finding her voice.

Doug smiled. "Of course. Xavier feels the same, don't you buddy?"

Xavier gave Selena a long, penetrating look and nodded. "I do."

After dabbing the corners of her mouth with her napkin, she placed it beside her plate. Selena had heard enough.

"Please excuse me, but I must use the ladies' room." Sliding out of the booth, Xavier stood up, Doug also rising to his feet, and watched her as she walked.

"Go after her, Xavier."

He turned and looked at Leandra. "What?"

"You just messed up — big time. Selena thinks you and Doug are serious."

"But . . . but we were joking."

"She doesn't know that, Xavier Eaton. Now, go after your woman before you lose her."

Galvanized into action, he wove his way

around several booths and banquettes until he stood at the door to the ladies' restroom. He tried the knob. The door was locked. "Selena?"

"Xavier?"

He pressed his ear against the door. "Yeah, baby. It's me."

"I am not your baby," she said from behind the door. "And get away from here before you're arrested."

"Open the door, Selena. I need to talk to you."

The door opened and before she could step out Xavier eased her back, closing and locking the door. "What are you doing? You're in the ladies' restroom."

He ignored her outburst, cradling her face in his hands. Light from a wall sconce fell across her face. There was something about her features that was so innocent, angelic, that it took his breath away.

"I'm sorry."

Her eyes narrowed. "Are you really, Xavier? Did you realize you sounded like a real idiot when you talk about your children addressing you as sir?"

"I know."

"If you know then why did you say it?"

He smiled. "It's something Doug, Bobby and me always joke about, but there's no way any of us would want our children to call us sir."

Embarrassed and angry because she'd been taken in, Selena made a fist and pounded his chest. "Ouch!" she gasped, shaking her hand. Hitting Xavier was like punching a brick wall.

Xavier caught her wrists while holding her arms against her sides. "Let's start over, Selena. I'm sorry about the joke. I like you. In fact I like you enough to want to see you again and again and again."

"Whoa! Hold up cowboy." Her eyes *and* mouth were smiling. "Have you forgotten that we just met yesterday?"

"No."

"No?" she repeated.

"I know I didn't stutter."

Selena struggled against his loose grip. "You're impossible."

"Why, Selena? Because I tell you that I like you?"

Selena struggled again, this time inwardly, her emotions vacillating between falling into Xavier's arms to tell him why she was reluctant to become involved, why she'd been forced to flee Los Angeles, or if she was thinking straight, tell him that this should be their first and last date.

"Please don't like me too much." The

entreaty tumbled off her lips, the admission as frightening as the danger that had dogged her.

Xavier cradled her face again. “I promise not to hurt you, Selena.”

She met his eyes, seeing tenderness and compassion in the dark orbs. There was no doubt he thought she was talking about a failed relationship when it was more — so much more than falling in and out of love.

What she’d found ironic was there was something about Xavier that reminded her of Derrick; her initial attraction to both men was instantaneous. Both were intelligent, charming and erudite. Her former lover had come from a prominent and influential African-American family with political ties spanning generations. Not only had she believed Derrick, but she had also trusted him. However, he’d violated that trust when he’d threatened her life.

Selena closed her eyes for several seconds. “Would you mind if we take it one day at a time? We’ll start with tonight and see what happens.”

Xavier saw vulnerability in Selena for the first time. “No, I don’t mind. I’ll go along with whatever you want.”

He prayed he hadn’t been coming on too strong, never having been that way with any other woman, but then Selena Yates wasn't any other woman. The women in his past were usually older. He'd discovered more mature women weren't into playing games. They said what was on their mind regardless of the consequence. Some had disclosed they were in the relationship for sex, while others wanted a liaison that would eventually lead to marriage.

"Whenever you plan something we need to talk about it together. I'm running a business."

Xavier was willing to agree to anything Selena proposed if only to continue to see her. He knew he was physically attracted to her, yet there was something else. And it was the something else he sought to uncover and understand. He'd been involved with some women who were incredibly beautiful, others very intelligent, and some witty and artistic, but Selena Yates was the only one who embodied all of these attributes. In his opinion, these attributes made her special.

"What day of the week is best for you?" he asked.

"Sunday."

"Is someone in there?" a woman called out on the other side of the door.

"We're coming out," Xavier shouted.

"Is there a man in there?" shrieked a woman.

A flash of humor crossed Selena's face. "You're busted, Xavier Eaton."

Taking her hand, Xavier turned, opened the door and led her out of the restroom, where a trio of women waited. Their expressions registered shock and amusement.

"Well, *damn!*" one spat out.

"That's what I'm talking about," another whispered.

"You may have ruined my reputation," Selena whispered when they were out of earshot of the women. "What if they were to come into Sweet Persuasions and recognize me?"

"I doubt if they'll recognize you without makeup and your head covered."

She narrowed her eyes at him. "Are you saying I usually look busted?"

"Nope. You just look different when you're working."

Selena was preempted from replying to his assessment of her when they arrived at their table. Douglas held Leandra, her head resting on his shoulder. "It's time I take Lee home."

"Is she all right?" Selena asked.

Smiling, Leandra opened her eyes. "I ate too much."

Xavier beckoned a waiter. Reaching into the pocket of his suit trousers, he removed a money clip and took out a large bill. The man put up his hands. "No, sir. Your order is on the house. That comes directly from Ms. Emma."

He tucked the bill into the waiter's shirt pocket. "That's your tip."

Douglas, who'd eased Leandra to sit up straight, reached into his pocket, taking out a bill. "And this is for the wine steward."

The waiter bowed from the waist. "Thank you. Thank you very much."

The two couples walked out of the restaurant as more were filing in. They'd spent more than two hours at Ma Bell's eating, drinking and, for Xavier, Douglas and Leandra, it had become a mini-reunion. The two men programmed their telephone numbers in each other's cell phones, while Selena promised Leandra that she would call her. She and the art teacher who was on maternity leave had exchanged numbers.

They left the Mayers in the restaurant's parking lot, walking hand-in-hand to where Xavier had parked his car. It appeared as if she'd just settled down on the leather seat when Selena found herself along the street behind her shop and apartment. She stared through the windshield. "I'm sorry if I overreacted back at the restaurant."

Xavier frowned. "What are you talking about?"

"You and Doug talking about your children calling you sir brought back bad childhood memories."

Shifting on his seat, he turned to stare at Selena's delicate profile. "What happened?"

Silence filled the car, swelling to enormous proportions as Selena gathered her thoughts. "A man who'd lived several houses from us had returned from the Gulf War with PTSD, demanding his wife call him sir. If she didn't, there was hell to pay. I don't know if he hit her, but there was always a lot of yelling. One day she left the house and didn't come back. What I couldn't understand was why she didn't take her children.

"His tirades continued and a couple of months later his son dropped out of school and took off. Sarah-Anne was too young to run away, so she escaped the only way she could. She waited for her father to go to sleep, then burned down the house with him in it. She was taken away by the police, and whenever I asked my parents about Sarah-Anne they said they didn't know."

"Did you believe them?" Xavier questioned.

Selena flashed a wry smile. "No. Only because I'd overhear them whispering about Sarah-Anne. I never discovered what happened to her, but wherever she is I hope she has found some peace."

Xavier tried to swallow to relieve the tightness in his throat. What he'd viewed as an innocent joke had triggered a traumatic memory from Selena's childhood. "I'm really sorry, Selena." He got out of the car and came around to assist her.

Unbuckling her belt, she placed her hand on his outstretched palm, he pulling her gently to stand. She met his eyes in the glow of a streetlight. "I had a wonderful evening. Thank you for making it special."

Xavier put his arm around her waist, pulling her to his length when four young men came down the block. They appeared to be college students that had too much to drink. One pushed another, and he stumbled and nearly fell into the roadway.

"I'll see you upstairs."

Selena shook her head. "It's all right I'll —"

"It's not all right," he said, cutting her off. "I'll see you to your door."

Opening her purse, Selena took out a set of keys. She wanted to tell Xavier that she was used to the antics of the many college students who lived for the weekends if only to release the frustrations of completing papers and cramming for exams. Although there was a door adjacent to the entrance to Sweet Persuasions and leading to the second-story apartments, she never entered through the front door. Even though she owned and operated the patisserie she didn't want her patrons to know where she lived. At first she'd thought she was being paranoid, but realized it made common sense not to advertise her residence.

She unlocked the door, stepping aside when Xavier pushed it open. He glanced up the staircase, then closed the door. Selena led the way up the stairs, feeling the heat of his gaze on her legs. "Going up and down these stairs several times a day doubles as a workout."

Xavier didn't respond as he watched the gentle sway of her hips in the fitted skirt. His gaze moved lower to her legs in the heels, wondering if Selena knew how sexy she was without even trying.

Selena opened the door to her apartment. Turning, she smiled up at Xavier. "Is this when I ask whether you'd like to come in for coffee?"

"Would you mind if I take a rain check?"

"Of course not." He'd passed the test. His

not wanting to come in meant she didn't have to fight off any unwanted advances. Xavier Eaton was back on her approval scale, and had moved up several notches. "I'm free Sunday afternoon." Selena wasn't certain where the admission had come from, but it was out and she couldn't retract it.

A slow, sensual grin found its way over Xavier's perfectly symmetrical masculine features, his mood buoyed by Selena's willingness to see him again. "Brunch at my place?"

"That sounds good," Selena repeated. "What time is brunch?"

"I'll pick you up at eleven."

Selena thought of her normal Sunday routine: attend church, put up several loads of laundry and clean her apartment. She'd tried keeping her daily schedule, but there were times she'd been forced to find the middle ground when something unexpected popped up. Last Saturday she didn't know Xavier Eaton existed, and now she was faced with the possibility of sharing brunch with a man who was a reminder that her past volatile relationship hadn't turned her off on the male species.

A mysterious smile softened her mouth. "May I bring dessert?"

Xavier angled his head, crossing his arms over his chest. "You may bring anything you want."

Going on tiptoe, Selena kissed his cheek. "Good night. I'll see you Sunday." She stepped inside the apartment and closed the door.

She was there, then she was gone. Xavier listened to the distinctive sound of the lock's deadbolt sliding into place before he retraced his steps. *You almost blew it, Eaton.*

It was apparent Selena wasn't amused by his joke that he'd demand his children address him as sir. It wasn't that she didn't have a sense of humor, because she laughed freely and easily. It was obvious Selena was more complex than she presented, and that was enough for him to hope for a relationship that went beyond sex.

Xavier sat up, reached over and flicked on the lamp on the bedside table. It had been hours since he'd dropped off Selena, yet he hadn't been able to fall asleep. He'd tossed and turned restlessly trying to will his mind blank, but to no avail. The images of her face, body and voice continued to assault him like traces of gunfire.

Walking on bare feet, he opened one of the many closets in the master bedroom.

When the architect had shown him the plans for the renovated interiors, he'd insisted on an abundance of storage and closet space. His bedroom had a wall of walk-in closets and another where he had stored his military paraphernalia.

Punching in the combination on a wall-installed safe, he opened the door and took out a key to a footlocker. Bending from the knees, he winced when he felt the slight twinge in the back of his calf. The occasional pain and discomfort was a constant reminder of what he referred to as an old war injury. It had been only nine months since his official discharge, but for Xavier it seemed more like nine days. Leaving the corps and teaching at Christopher Munroe had eased the transition from active military to civilian military.

He opened the locker, removing the leather pouch and several pairs of white gloves he'd worn during military parades and weddings. He'd put off reading the journals because he hadn't expected to see Bobby Bell or visit his family-owned restaurant with Selena Yates. His initial weekend plans included reading the journals, doing lesson plans and, weather permitting, relaxing on the chaise at the rear of the house. Although many of the rooms in the house were empty, the exterior of the property had been completed. A landscaper had revived a flower garden, put in a number of fruit and palmetto trees and the newly seeded lawn spouted grass that resembled green carpet.

A number of handguns, including an antique derringer with a decoratively carved gold-plated handle and his dress military sword were in the footlocker. A wooden case with his medals, wrapped in felt shown through a large plastic bag. Everything in the locker represented a time and a place in his life that would never be repeated. There were soldiers who'd returned to combat after losing one or both legs, but Xavier having his leg shattered while looking at death, when the Afghan stood over him ready to end his life had been the third strike. He'd promised his parents, his mother in particular, that if he sustained a third injury he would resign his commission. Fortunately he'd lived to keep the promise. The clock on the fireplace mantel softly chimed the hour. It was one in the morning and he was prowling around the half-empty house like a vampire.

Xavier secured the locker and returned the key to the safe. He got into bed, slipped on the gloves. Opening the leather pouch, he removed one of the tattered, cloth-covered journals and began reading the one with the earliest dated entry:

> Property of Josiah Baruch Chadburn. If found return to Chadburn Plantation, Johns Island, South Carolina. — 1 January 1858.
> I was born 27 February in the year of our Lord 1841 the only issue to Malvina, house slave and her owner James Jacob Chadburn. People say she was her master's favorite slave and she made him promise any children they would have together would be born free.

Xavier smiled. It was apparent Malvina used her favored status to ensure her child would not be a slave. Reaching across his body he picked up a pen and pad, jotting down notes. Charlotte Burke wouldn't divulge the name of the woman who'd given her pouch, but now he didn't need her name. He had the name of the owner of the journals and the plantation on which he'd been born. It was easy enough for him to research the plantation if it was listed on the National Register of Historic Places, and the courthouse for census records, validating Josiah Chadburn. He curbed the urge to get his laptop and go online as he continued reading:

Mama died in 1852 and so did my sister who I am told was stillborn. Folks say Mr. Chadburn never recovered from losing her. Colored folks say Mama put a spell on him where he would only have babies with her or he could not love another woman. Mr. Chadburn married after Mama died and had four babies with his new wife. Slaves always talk too much.

After spending more than fifteen years in Europe where Mr. Chaburn said I would have a quality education, I came home today.

April 1858 — the Democratic National Convention was held in Charleston. Delegates from the Cotton States walked out of the meeting when Stephen Douglas took the lead.

Politics is the only topic of discussion amongst free folks and slaves. There is talk about the suppression of the African slave trade, admitting Kansas to the United States as a free state and a homestead act to open land for new settlers in the West. I talked to Mr. Chadburn about going West, but he said he wants me to go to Boston to continue my education.

Xavier continued to read the entries that spanned another three years; most of them terse sentences or an occasional paragraph wherein Josiah wrote of his frustration of being a free man but not feeling free whenever someone questioned his citizenship. He'd graduated college and was on his way home when he'd been stopped in Virginia; he hadn't had his papers attesting to his free status; he'd spent three days in a Fredericksburg jail until John Chadburn sent someone to pay his fine and escort him back to South Carolina.

Although educated as an engineer, Josiah's focus was politics. Topics like slavery, states' rights and the talk of secession had consumed him. There was a brief entry about a possible marriage with a young Negro woman whom he'd met in Boston, but the nuptials were postponed when Southern delegates met February 4, 1861 at Montgomery, Alabama, to form the Confederate States of America. Jefferson Davis was chosen president and Alexander H. Stephens of Georgia as vice president.

Xavier turned the page. He picked up a daguerreotype of a young woman dressed in the height of mid-nineteenth-century fashion. The photo was no doubt that of Josiah Chadburn's intended. The petite woman was dark in coloring, but very pretty. She reminded Xavier of the beautiful black dolls in his sister's doll collection. He wanted to know if Josiah ever married Miss Hannah Shaw, but his eyes were tired, vision blurring. Closing the journal, he returned it to the pouch and pulled off the gloves. A quick glance at the clock on the mantelpiece indicated it was after three-thirty.

This time when Xavier turned off the lamp and closed his eyes he fell asleep. It was hours later that he began to dream. First there were images of the horrors he'd experienced during combat, then they segued to vivid pictures based on the entries in Josiah Chadburn's journal.

He knew the journals were authentic because Josiah was familiar with names and places known only to someone who'd witnessed it firsthand, or how else would he have known that Fernando Wood was the mayor of New York City at that time?

The images faded and he fell into a deep dreamless sleep, and when he woke, the bedside telephone was ringing and the bright sunlight was pouring into the bedroom through the sheers. Pushing into a sitting position, he picked the cordless instrument off the cradle.

"Hello."

"Did I wake you?" said a familiar male voice.

"Not really," he half lied. Xavier was glad the phone had rang because one of his pet peeves was sleeping late. "What's up, Doug?"

"I'm calling to give you a heads up about next Sunday."

"What's going on?"

"I've been in contact with some of the guys from school, and they're coming over in the afternoon for a cookout at my place. They're bringing their wives and girlfriends, so I thought you'd like to come with Selena."

Running a hand over his face, Xavier breathed out an inaudible sigh. There was no doubt either Bobby or Doug had called to round up the cadets from their graduating class. It had been a while since he'd connected with any of them.

"I'm game, but I don't know about Selena. I'm not certain what she has planned for that afternoon." He remembered her saying he had to check with her before making plans that included both of them.

"Can't you get her to change her plans?" Doug asked.

Xavier wanted to tell his former classmate that his relationship with Selena, if there was to be one, was too new for him to try and pressure her into rearranging her life for him. After all, she'd reminded him that they'd only met a couple of days ago.

"I don't know, Doug. You know how women can be once they set their minds to something."

"Look buddy, I'll keep you out of this. I'll have Lee get in touch with her. I'm certain she can talk her into coming."

"If your wife can't convince her, then no one can."

"You've got that right," Doug said in agreement. "There's a running joke that Lee can sell snow to Eskimos. She was so sick the first four months that she was afraid to leave the house because of nausea. Now that she's feeling better she says she's ready to party."

"I'll be there even if Selena doesn't make it."

Xavier ended the call, swung his legs over the side of the bed and headed for the en suite bathroom. Douglas, assigned to the Parris Island Marine Corps Recruit Deport, commuted between Charleston and Beaufort because his wife refused to live on base. She'd complained of feeling like a gypsy every time her father was transferred from one state or country to another.

It was the possibility of not knowing where he would be transferred or assigned that precluded Xavier from taking whatever relationship he'd had with a woman to another level. He'd changed and the turn his life had taken had also changed. He'd returned to Charleston to put down roots and start anew. Xavier didn't know what the future held for him, but there was a reason why his life had been spared. And that meant he had to make the most of what he'd been given, and that was a second chance.

Chapter 6

"Good morning, Sweet Persuasions." Selena made it a habit to answer the phone before the second ring. Her telephone and internet service had been restored, and while foot traffic was slow her online orders had increased. If the online orders continued faster than her retail sales, then she seriously thought about going completely mail order.

"Hey, Selena. This is Lee."

"Hi. What's up?"

"First I want to invite you to come to my place for a backyard cookout next Sunday afternoon. And I also want to order enough dessert for at least twenty to twenty-five people. Can you help me out with that?"

Selena smiled. "You're in luck, because whenever I put together something for Ma Bell's Sunday Gospel Brunch I have extra, so I'll set some aside for you."

"Thanks. Are you coming with Xavier?"

Her smile faded. "Is he invited?"

"Of course he is. Hasn't he called you?"

"No. Don't worry. I'll call him."

"I told everyone to come around two. Is that time good for you?" Leandra asked.

"It's fine." By two she would've gone to church, cleaned her apartment and put up several loads of wash. Selena ended the call, then reached into the pocket of her apron for her cell, scrolling through the directory for Xavier's number. It wasn't until it had rung twice that she went completely still. She'd volunteered to call Xavier asking him to go with her when he may have committed to taking another woman.

"Yes, Selena."

She jumped slightly when hearing the deep voice come through the earpiece. "How did you know it was me?"

"Your name came up on the display."

"Oh?"

"Oh, what, baby?"

"I . . . I want to know if you would go with me to Doug and Lee's cookout next Sunday." Xavier's laugh caressed her ear.

"Are you asking me out on a date, Ms. Yates?"

She sucked her teeth loud enough for him to hear. "I did tell you that I'd call you whenever I had some free time. And, it just so happens that I'm usually free Sunday afternoons. Now, if you don't want to come with me, then I'll just have to ask someone else." Selena wouldn't tell him there wasn't anyone she'd want to accompany her but him.

There was a pregnant pause before Xavier's voice came through the earpiece again. "I can't believe you called to ask me to go out with you, then in the same breath you mention going with another man. I thought we were a couple."

She smiled. "I didn't know it had gone *that* far, Xavier."

"You bet it has. Last night was a test run. It's like going to a car dealer for a test drive. If you happen to like the car then you buy it. If not, either you test drive another one or give up. Yours truly decided the test drive was worth buying."

This time it was Selena who was momentarily rendered speechless. "I can't believe you would compare me to a damn car!"

Xavier laughed softly. "Don't get snippy, darling. It was just an analogy. And, if you were a car, then you would definitely be a Rolls or a Bentley."

"Oh, now you're trying to clean it up."

"No, Selena. One thing I don't do is apologize for what I say. If I tell you that I like you it's because I do. And if I tell you that I *want* you it is also because I do. I hope you understand where I'm coming from?"

Her eyelids fluttered. Xavier could not have been more forthcoming. "I don't believe you've given me much of a choice."

"If you have any doubts, then I'll be certain to give you a special in-home demonstration."

"What?!"

"I'll show you when I see you tomorrow. Bye, baby."

She stood holding the tiny instrument to her ear until she realized that Xavier had hung up. Who, she mused, had she become involved with? The bell over the door jangled and she looked up to see a well-dressed woman in a tailored, black-silk pantsuit and a blonde teen. The girl was a walking billboard for the more popular clothing labels targeted for teens.

"Good morning," Selena said in greeting. "Welcome to Sweet Persuasions."

The woman flashed a friendly smile. "Thank you. My friend recommended your shop and I'd like to know if it's possible for you to cater a chocolate dessert party."

Selena gestured to a bistro table. "Please sit down." She pulled over a chair from another table, sat and extended her hand.

"I'm Selena Yates." The woman with pale skin, startling sky-blue eyes and a stylish salt-and-pepper coif shook her hand.

"I'm Janice Pernell, and this my granddaughter, Carrie. We're hosting a little celebration for her thirteenth birthday, October 2 at six in the evening, and instead of a cake she wants chocolate desserts."

"How many guests are you expecting, Mrs. Pernell?"

"There will be twenty children and at least thirty adults. All totaled I don't think there will be more than fifty."

"What if I make enough for sixty?"

Janice smiled. "That sounds good."

Selena turned her attention to the girl who stared at her with large, dark gray eyes. "Do you have an idea of what you want?"

Carrie lifted her shoulders under a rose-pink sweatshirt. "Not really."

"Mrs. Pernell, would you mind if I make some suggestions?" Selena asked. The older woman shook her head. "I could put together a combination of fresh fruit covered in chocolate."

"What kind of fruit?" Carrie asked.

"Bananas, strawberries, mandarin oranges and kiwi."

Carrie smiled for the first time. "I like those."

Selena returned her smile. "Good." She'd hoped she wouldn't have to deal with a surly teenager. "I can also make a variety of molded candies with nuts and fruit, flavored truffles and if you have a favorite animal I can use chocolate to make it into a display or a centerpiece."

"I like clowns," Carrie said quickly, then scrunched up her nose. "Is a clown too hard to make?"

Selena shook her head, her mind spinning with what she would have to use to fashion a chocolate clown. "No." She usually made sketches of her designs before using molding chocolate. "The ingredients in molding chocolate aren't meant to be eaten, so I'll make you several smaller edible chocolate rabbits."

"Grandma, can I have chocolate rabbits as party favors?"

Janice tugged playfully at her granddaughter's ponytail. "I told you if you got a very good report card you could have anything you want, dear."

Selena's expression softened as she watched the interchange between grandmother and granddaughter, reminding her of her own close relationship with her Grandma Lily. She'd promised her grandmother and other family members she would come up to visit with them over the Thanksgiving weekend.

"What about the adults, Mrs. Pernell? Would you also like desserts for them?"

"Yes. And please call me Janice."

"I can make a Black Forest cherry cake, mousse under a chocolate icing, or a raspberry cream torte. There is also a Sacher torte, which is the symbol of Viennese confectionery, that's usually a big hit at parties."

Janice angled her head as if deep in thought. "I'd love for you to add some chocolate candies. Even though I shouldn't eat it, I love chocolate fudge." She opened her handbag and took out an envelope. "I believe there is enough in here to pay for whatever you decide to make. I've also included a business card with the information where everything should be delivered."

Selena took the envelope without examining its contents. "I will make up and label a tray without nuts or chocolate for those who may have allergies."

A flush crept over Janice's face, giving it an attractive warm glow. "I was so busy running off at the mouth that I'd forgotten about food allergies."

"It's okay, because that is something I always discuss with my clients."

Janice smoothed down the front of her jacket. "I believe that does it."

Selena smiled. "I'll be in touch with you a day before the delivery, so you can see what I've done. If at that time you want something else, I will have an extra day to make it."

"You're the professional and the expert, Ms. Yates. Whatever you make, I am certain will be simply divine." Janice stood up, her granddaughter following suit. "I look forward to hearing from you."

Selena rose and walked them to the door. She stood, staring through the glass. A liveried chauffer had opened the rear door to a top-of-the-line Mercedes-Benz sedan for Janice and Carrie. It was only after the driver had driven away from the curb that she opened the envelope and counted the contents. Mrs. Janice Pernell had given her enough money to offset the rent for the patisserie and her apartment for the next three months. Turning over the business card, she stared at the raised lettering. The address where she would deliver her chocolates was located on South Battery.

When she'd first moved to the city she'd set aside Sunday afternoons for a walking tour of different neighborhoods. It had been the majestic homes and mansions on South

Battery that had held her rapt attention. She'd stood by, listening to a tour guide explain to a group of tourists that the rise of cotton in the eighteenth century as the South's biggest cash crop issued in a new era of wealth for Charlestonians. With their newfound wealth, planters and shipping merchants built opulent fashionable town houses on South Battery, using the finest materials available at that time.

Selena felt a warm glow of pride and satisfaction flow through her. Whenever she'd taken on a project, whether it was decorating her dollhouse or studying and rehearsal for a role, she'd always given it everything she had.

And it was no different when she sat down to make her chocolate concoctions. It was during the cross-country drive that she'd spent hours planning the next phase of her life. She'd stopped in a small restaurant in Utah where she'd ordered chocolate mousse. When she raved to the waitress about the dessert the woman gave her the recipe. Once she was settled into her apartment over the vacant shop that would eventually become Sweet Persuasions, Selena retrieved the recipe and made the mousse. It'd come out deliciously and sinfully decadent. She'd always been an adequate cook, but it was her ability to bake that had given her the most satisfaction. She re-created the mousse over and over, adding brownies and cheesecake to her baking repertoire. It took a month of making desserts for Selena to decide that she wanted to become a pastry chef.

Going online, she'd researched pastry schools in the area and registered for a six-month course. After receiving her certificate, she'd signed on for another course to study under a master confectioner. She read everything she could about starting up a small business and a year after she'd come to call Charleston home she opened Sweet Persuasions. And despite working long hours, having little or no personal time for herself, she loved what she did.

Taking a block of raw chocolate and turning it into edible art had become more rewarding than acting. As an actress her goal was to make people believe the character she was portraying. As the owner of Sweet Persuasions she could be herself.

Selena stood outside Sweet Persuasions waiting for Xavier to arrive. She, who'd lived in Charleston for eighteen months hadn't had a single date before Xavier Eaton walked into the patisserie. Not one date and only one friend: Monica Mills.

If she hadn't had to leave L.A. her social calendar would've been filled with parties and award-show and movie appearances. The highlight of her career had been what dress and/or jewelry to wear on the red carpet. Before she'd dated Derrick exclusively, she'd had a merry-go-round of dates. Most of them were pre-arranged by her publicist with the intent to enhance her image and those of the young men whose looks far exceeded their talent.

On the set, professional makeup and haute couture had transformed her from ordinary to extraordinary. The transformation was complete when Selena Yates became Raina Vaughan. Her manager felt Raina sounded more theatrical than Selena, and her portrayal of the bitchy illegitimate mixed-race daughter of the town's wealthiest man had made her character a viewer favorite.

A silver sports car maneuvered up alongside the curb, the engine humming like a contented feline. Selena was smiling when Xavier unfolded his tall frame, got out and, taking long strides, closed the distance between them. Her stomach muscles made a crazy flip-flop motion as she sucked air into her lungs in an attempt to calm her runaway pulse. She wasn't certain whether she preferred him in the tailored suit he'd worn for date night or the relaxed jeans, golf shirt and running shoes. He'd covered his cropped hair with a black baseball cap.

Selena extended her arms and she wasn't disappointed when Xavier folded her in his embrace, molding her body to his length. Pressing a kiss to his smooth jaw, she buried her face against the column of his strong neck. "How are you?"

Xavier turned his head slightly, brushing a kiss over her mouth, a kiss that had become a caress. "Wonderful."

Selena was like a breath of fresh air. Soft waves framed her face and the light cover of makeup enhanced her best features. She'd chosen to wear a pair of black cropped cotton pants, a white, man-tailored, three-quarter-sleeve shirt and black leather ballet-type flats. He glanced down at the large shopping bag at her feet. "Are you taking the bag?"

"Yes. It's dessert."

Cupping her elbow, Xavier directed Selena around to the Porsche to the driver's side. Bending slightly, he opened the door. "Get in baby."

"What?"

He leaned in close. "You're going to drive to my house."

Selena stared at Xavier over her shoulder. "I don't know how to get there." He gave her the address. "You really want me to drive your car?"

"I can't tell you what I really want you to do, but yes I want you to drive."

She slipped in behind the wheel, adjusted the seat to accommodate her shorter legs and secured the seat belt, while Xavier got in beside her. Driving the Porsche would be very different from her four-year-old minivan. She'd traded in her two-seater Audi for the minivan to transport her chocolate creations.

Signaling, she adjusted the mirrors, and then pulled out into traffic once she saw an opening. "I like this car," she crooned, taking a right at the next intersection.

Reclining his seat, Xavier closed his eyes and crossed his arms over his chest. "I like it, too." He'd asked Selena to drive because he was exhausted. He'd stayed up late again reading Josiah Chadburn's journal, alternating taking notes with researching facts online. The sun was up when he finally closed the journal, turned off his laptop and fell into a deep sleep. If he hadn't gotten a telephone call from Bobby there was no doubt he would still be asleep.

"Xavier?"

"Yes, baby."

"Do you mind if I turn on the radio?"

"No."

Selena switched on the satellite radio station featuring music from the '90s. She then gave Xavier a quick glance. He'd pulled his cap down over his face. "Are you going to sleep on me?"

"I'm taking a power nap."

"Didn't you sleep last night?"

"Not much."

"What were you doing?"

Xavier pushed back the cap. "Reading."

Selena stopped at a red light. "You were reading until what time?"

"I think it was around six o'clock when I finally fell asleep."

"And what time did you wake up?"

"I don't know, Selena."

She gave him a dark, layered look. "I'm sorry if I'm bothering you, but what good are you going to be with little or no sleep?" If he'd gone to sleep at six and he'd picked her up at eleven, then that meant he hadn't had more than a few hours of sleep.

Signaling, she pulled over to the right at an intersection, waited for cars to pass, then executed a U-turn. She knew if she went to Xavier's house he would probably go to bed and she wouldn't be able to get back home unless she called a taxi. "We're going back to my place. What do you say to that, Xavier?" Snoring greeted her pronouncement. She gave him an incredulous stare. He had fallen asleep.

Xavier had changed positions, his head resting at an odd angle, his breathing slower and deeper. Watching him as he slept offered Selena the advantage of staring at him without censoring herself. He was so incredibly handsome she wondered why some woman hadn't claimed him as her husband. He'd admitted he liked women, but somehow he'd managed to remain a bachelor.

Selena had to circle the block behind the shop twice before she found an empty space close to her building. She shook Xavier in an attempt to wake him. He mumbled, shifted position, but didn't open his eyes.

She shook him again, this time harder. "Wake up, Xavier!"

Xavier opened his eyes, arms flailing wildly. "What! What!" His eyelids fluttered as he tried focusing on the face inches from his own. "Where are we?"

"You're back at my place."

Reaching up, he adjusted his cap. "I thought we were going to my house."

"Get out of the car, Xavier."

He blinked once. "What?"

"You heard what I said. Get out of the car." Selena had enunciated each word.

Xavier did not move. "Where are we going?"

Selena pushed her face close to his. "Upstairs."

His eyebrows lifted. "What are *we* going to do upstairs?"

"*We* are going to bed," she countered.

"You're kidding?"

Her eyes narrowed. "Do I look like I'm kidding? Now, please get out of the car."

Selena didn't tell Xavier that he was going to bed — alone. And when he woke, then he would drive home — alone. If she allowed him to get behind the wheel and drive off and he'd hurt himself or killed someone because he'd dozed off she would live with the guilt for the rest of her life.

Xavier opened the door, following Selena into her apartment building. Holding on to the banister, he made it up the staircase, feeling as if he'd drunk too much when he hadn't had anything alcoholic since he'd gone to Ma Bell's.

Selena unlocked the door, stepping aside and beckoning him. "Come on in."

She led him down a hallway, passing the kitchen, laundry room and pantry and into her bedroom. Her initial plan to turn the second bedroom into one for guests was scrapped after she decided the space was better suited for a workroom. There was a drafting table where she sketched her confectionery designs and a wall of shelves was filled with books and plastic bins with materials for her needle craft projects and another lined with sweetgrass baskets. A comfortable chaise with a matching ottoman was positioned to take advantage of the early morning sun, and the only piece of electronic equipment was an audio system. Listening to music while she sketched or knitted was the balm Selena needed for total relaxation.

Xavier walked into the bedroom, stopping short. The near all-white space was feminine and inviting. Crocheted panels covering the tall narrow windows matched the tablecloth on a round table with two pull-up chairs and the canopy on a bleached pine four-poster bed.

"This room is beautiful."

"Thank you." Reaching for his hand, Selena pulled Xavier over to a white-wicker cushioned rocking chair. "Please take off your clothes and get into bed."

"Where are you going?" he asked, covering a yawn with his hand when she turned and walked to the door.

She stopped, winking at him over her shoulder. "I have to do something. I'll be back."

Selena knew the moment Xavier's head touched the pillow he would fall asleep again. In fact she was counting on it. If he didn't, then she would find herself in a quandary. She'd invited a man she hadn't known a week to sleep under her roof who probably expected her to make love with him. If she were honest with herself, then she would've admitted she not only wanted Xavier Eaton, but she also needed to belong to him.

Xavier tried, but he couldn't keep his eyes open as he dropped down to the rocker, watching Selena until she disappeared from his line of vision. He didn't want to want her — but he did. He'd told himself that she was much too serious for someone her age, and it was her age that had given him pause. He liked older women and although he was cognizant of the seven-year difference in their ages, her being younger made him want to protect her. He'd tried analyzing why she didn't want him to like her too much; could it be she didn't believe in love, or maybe a failed relationship had made her overly cautious.

Xavier had never gone into a relationship with a woman looking for love. Even when a few women had professed being in love with him he did not return their declaration with one of his own. One thing he refused to do was lie and he'd never confused liking with loving. If or when he fell in love he would know it *and* he knew he wouldn't hesitate to let the woman on the receiving end know what lay in his heart.

He'd grown up watching his father caress his mother when he thought no one was looking. It was something as simple as Boaz resting his hand on Paulette's back, or leaning in to kiss her hair. The gestures were tender and deliberate. When he'd asked his father what signs he had to look for to know that he'd fallen in love with a woman, Boaz's comeback was if he were willing to give up everything he had — and that included his life — for her. His dad went on to remind him that love was giving, caring, sharing, peaceful and most of all quiet.

Kicking off his running shoes, he removed his socks, then jeans. He stripped down to bare skin, folding the clothes neatly and leaving them on the rocker. His feet were silent as a cat's on the plush off-white area rug as he made his way to the bed. He pulled back the coverlet, a quilt and slipped between cool, scented sheets. The bed was like the woman who slept there: it beckoned him to come *and* stay awhile.

CHAPTER 7

Opening the door to the eye-level oven, Selena checked the small turkey for doneness. Twenty minutes after she'd left Xavier she'd returned to the bedroom to find him sprawled on the bed on his back, sleeping soundly. Knowing he would be asleep for a while, she'd gone into the kitchen to prepare Sunday dinner. She always cooked more than she needed; the extra portions would serve as lunch and dinner leftovers for several days.

The telephone rang, and she reached for the receiver before it woke Xavier. "Hello."

"Hello, neighbor. I'm calling to invite you to come over for dinner."

Selena settled on a tall stool at the cooking island. "I can't, Monica."

"I brought back some of my mama's pot roast."

"You know I love your mother's pot roast, but I'm going to have to decline."

"Why do you sound so different? Do you have company?"

"Yes, I do, Ms. Mills." Her voice was barely a whisper. "We'll talk tomorrow."

"And you better tell me everything," Monica threatened. "Well, almost everything.

"Hang up, Ms. M."

Frowning, Selena depressed the button, ending the call. Did she really sound that different? And did her sounding different have anything to do with the man sleeping under her roof.

Working in the kitchen while Xavier slept had her contemplating what-ifs. What if they were a couple? What if she were to play house with a man whose very presence disturbed her physically and emotionally? A man who made her feel things she'd long forgotten. The night before she'd had an erotic dream, and when she woke she found the area between her legs wet and pulsing. Interacting with Xavier Eaton had reminded her she didn't want or need any man as much as she wanted and needed *him.*

Selena had lingered in bed, mentally replaying the past few years of her life. She'd fled L.A., hiding out in Charleston where she felt safe. She was a small-business owner who'd managed to keep a low profile, while she had to decide when her one-year lease expired whether to go completely mail order.

Her love life was nonexistent, her social life lukewarm before Xavier walked into Sweet Persuasions. They had exchanged kisses that bordered on chaste but that hadn't stopped her from wanting more. And the "more" translated into making love with Xavier. It no longer mattered if she'd known him a day, week, a month or even a year. She wanted the man!

Her phone rang again, this time it was her cell. She glanced at the display before hitting the talk button. "Hi, Lee."

"Hey, Selena."

"What's up?"

"I should've asked you when I called yesterday but . . ."

"But what, Lee?"

"Do you have any free time when we could hang out together? Most of the women I'd gone to college with have either moved away or . . ." Her voice trailed off again.

It wasn't what Leandra Mayer said, but what she hadn't said. Selena knew she'd taken a leave from her teaching position and she and Doug had recently moved into a house in a neighborhood known as Sandhurst. Not only was Lee bored, but also lonely.

"What about tomorrow? After I do my banking, I'm free for the rest of the morning."

"I'll treat you to breakfast, then we can go on a shopping spree. I still have to pick out furniture for the nursery."

"Do you mind if we leave shopping for another time?" Selena asked. "Monday afternoon is when I do most of my baking for the week."

"No problem. Should I expect you tomorrow?"

Selena smiled, although Leandra couldn't see her. "Yes."

She ended the call and set the phone on the cooking island. It had become feast or famine. In four days her social circle had expanded from Monica Mills to Xavier Eaton, Douglas and Leandra Mayer and Robert Bell. Bobby she knew because she supplied desserts for his family-owned business but her interaction with him had been business-based.

She glanced at the clock on the microwave. Xavier had been asleep for more than four hours. Hopping off the stool, she adjusted the oven's temperature when she heard movement behind her. Selena turned to find Xavier at the entrance to the kitchen, arms crossed over his bare chest. Seeing him wearing nothing but a pair of jeans riding low on his slim hips sent her libido into overdrive. His upper body was as magnificent as his face. Her gaze was drawn to the colorful tattoo over his heart. The anchor, globe and eagle superimposed on an American flag with Semper Fi and USMC identified him as a member of the corps.

A hint of a smile played around his mouth as he sniffed the air like a large cat. "I smell turkey."

"You've got a good nose," she confirmed. "Are you staying for dinner?"

"But of course. How much time do we have before we eat?"

Selena glanced at the clock again. "Probably forty minutes."

"I thought you were coming to bed with me." There was a hint of laughter in his voice.

She assumed a similar position, crossing her arms under her breasts. "You were sleeping so soundly that I didn't have the heart to wake you."

Xavier walked into the kitchen, shaking his head as he approached the woman who'd changed into a pair of shorts and tank top. "You're not slick, baby."

Selena's arms came down, she giving him

a look that screamed innocence. She knew she'd been found out, but she wasn't about to admit that to him. It was situations such as this one she'd found herself in that her theatrical training served her well.

"I really don't know what you're talking about, Xavier."

He stood less than a foot away. "You had no intention of getting into bed with me, did you?"

"Why would you say that?" Xavier had pushed his hands into the pockets of his jeans pulling the low-rise waistband down to where it was obvious he wasn't wearing underwear. Selena's composure nearly slipped when she saw a tuft of pubic hair.

"I know I was a little tired, but if you had awakened me I probably would've gone right back to sleep."

Reaching out, Selena rested her palms over his hard pectorals. "I'm sorry, darling, if you believe I deceived you."

"Oh. Now I'm your darling?"

"If I'm your baby, then why can't you be my darling? Or would you prefer to be *my boo?*"

Xavier went completely still. He didn't know whether Selena was acting or if she was being truthful. After all, she'd admitted she'd been an actress. He took a step, pulling her flush against his length, molding their bodies from chest to thigh. Staring at her staring up at him, Xavier's eyes caressed her face. "I don't have a problem being your darling, boo or any other term of endearment, *baby.*" He drew out the last word.

A rush of heat swept over Selena's face, and she lowered her gaze. Xavier was making love to her with his eyes. "Did you sleep well?"

A corner of his firm mouth tilted in a half smile. Xavier knew Selena was a little uncomfortable with the turn the conversation had taken. "Like a newborn."

He lowered his head and kissed her. It wasn't just lips touching, but a caress communicating tenderness, trust and protection. What he felt whenever he was with Selena was so different from the other women in his past that he felt slightly off balance. With them it had been lust and unbridled sex, but with her it went beyond his wanting to be inside her.

Moaning in frustration, Selena's arms went under Xavier's shoulders as she sought to get closer. Being in his arms, having him kiss her was a reminder of her prolonged period of self-imposed celibacy. She was a normal woman with physical urges that needed to be assuaged, yet she'd rejected the advances of every man who'd appeared to take an interest in her. There were times when she'd wished she could engage in a one-night stand, but the opportunity had never presented itself — until now. She was certain she could sleep with Xavier and not have any regrets.

Xavier felt the rush of breath from Selena's parted lips as she threw back her head and bared her throat. He fastened his mouth to the base of her throat, his tongue flicking over the smooth scented skin; his tongue moved upward, tracing a path along the column of her neck, starting with her ear to the curve of a bare shoulder.

Anchoring his hands under the straps of the tank top, he eased them off her shoulders, exposing firm breasts to his hungry gaze. Without warning, it happened. A fireball exploded in his groin and with it came an instantaneous erection. Bending slightly, Xavier picked Selena up and carried her effortlessly into the bedroom. He placed her on the unmade bed, his body following hers down, before rolling over to lie beside her.

There was no way he would make love to Selena without protection. Shifting on his side, he reached over and pulled her to face him, staring deeply into her eyes. "What do you want?" he whispered as if he feared being overhead, although they were the only two in the room.

Selena felt the prick of hot tears behind her eyelids. Xavier was asking a question to which she had no answer. She couldn't tell him that she wanted him to love her, love her enough where she could forget that all men weren't crazy; men who turned into obsessive monsters seeking to destroy anything denied them rather than walk away.

Closing her eyes in an attempt to stem the flow of tears, she said, "I need you." The admission came from somewhere she didn't know existed.

"Open your eyes, baby." She complied, her eyes shimmering with unshed tears. "I promise you this is not going to be a hit it and quit it."

She pulled her top over her breasts before placing her fingertips to his mouth. "You don't have to promise anything. I stopped expecting promises once I grew up."

Xavier flashed a wide grin. Selena was right. She was grown. Grown and sexy. Without warning, he sobered. "Why don't you want me to like you too much?"

A beat passed. "I dated a guy who went psycho on me when I told him we needed to stop seeing so much of each other."

"Were you living together?"

"No," she said.

"How long were you seeing each other?"

Selena drew in a breath, held it, then exhaled slowly. She had to tell Xavier about her relationship with Derrick, rid herself of the emotional baggage she'd been carrying around, even if she'd refused to acknowledge it. "Not quite two years. An acquaintance introduced me to him and — the attraction — we hit if off immediately."

"Were you acting at the time?" Xavier questioned when Selena fell silent. Resting an arm over her hip, he pulled her close.

"Yes." Selena closed her eyes rather than watching for Xavier's reaction. "I was working on a movie and had several speaking parts in what they call 'special business.' They were never more than one or two lines, but they were credits I added to my résumé. I'd made a few commercials and every time they aired I received a residual. The monies I earned from commercials paid the rent and kept the wolf from the door.

"My star began to rise when I landed a supporting role in a made-for-television movie. It was family-rated drama aired on the Hallmark Channel. The director told me about an audition for a daytime soap, promising to put in a good word for me. I read for the part of a mixed-race illegitimate daughter of the town's wealthiest man. The role called for a bitch and I must have been very convincing because the head writer and director hired me on the spot."

Xavier listened intently. Her manager had suggested she legally change her name to Raina Vaughn, but she'd refused, using the latter as her stage name. She was given a stylist who'd transformed her from small-town, fresh-faced college student to Hollywood glam. Her so-called love life was staged by her publicist, she walking the red carpet with men who competed with her when it came to who was more beautiful.

Her expression and voice changed when she talked about a man who'd literally swept her off her feet. She admitted he was a breath of rarified air when she'd compared him to the vapid male actors and models hoping for their big break.

"I felt as if I was on top of the world when I signed a one-year contract for a daytime drama. I moved out of the apartment I'd been sharing, and into a furnished studio apartment not far from Hollywood Hills. My relationship with Derrick was as close to perfect as I could've imagined it could be. He was generous, attentive, came from a prominent L.A. family and had impeccable manners. It was obvious I was looking through the proverbial rose-colored glasses because I'd refused to see that my so-called perfect boyfriend had become obsessive and jealous.

"He complained whenever I had an on-screen kiss with another actor, or if the studio paired me with a costar for soap-related promotions. After a while I felt smothered, he wasn't allowing me to breathe. He'd come to the studio, but when he was denied access he began waiting for me outside my apartment building. His excuse was he was bringing me food because I was working too hard and not eating enough."

"Was that true?" Xavier asked.

Selena closed her eyes for several seconds. "No. Actors eat well whether it is at a studio or on location. When I finally worked up enough nerve to tell him that I couldn't see him during the week because I had to memorize at least fifty pages of script every time I stepped in front of the camera, he went ballistic."

Xavier's expression changed, becoming a mask of stone. "Did he hit you?"

"No. He shocked me when he began crying and couldn't stop. He finally pulled himself together and walked out. I didn't see him for a couple of weeks, and when he showed up outside the studio it was as if nothing had occurred. He agreed with my suggestion we see each other on the weekends. This arrangement seemed to work until he called to tell me he needed to see some people and take care of a problem."

"What did he do for a living?"

"He is a partner in a family-owned business. This time I didn't see him for about three months. I vacillated between calling his father and doing nothing. After all, I was the one who wanted for us to deescalate."

"What did you do?" Xavier had asked another question.

"I did nothing. This must have fueled his rage, because when he showed up again he accused me of not loving him — not caring whether he lived or died. First, I didn't recognize him because he looked as if he was homeless. When I asked him if he'd taken care of his problem, his comeback was he was the problem. He'd gone away to find himself. I wanted to tell him that he'd left unstable and returned crazy. There was a look in his eyes that scared the hell out of me, so I told him to leave and not come back.

"That's when the stalking began. I'd find

him sitting in a car across the street from my apartment building whenever I left or returned. He began showing up at the studio, knowing he would be denied access. It all came to a head when he made a scene after I'd come out of a restaurant with an actor who'd been selected as my on-screen love interest. It escalated into a shouting match, and I told my costar to leave because I didn't want him involved in something that could possibly derail his career. Derrick waited for Manuel to drive out of the parking lot, then put a knife to my throat, threatening if he couldn't have me then no man would."

Tears Selena had held in check overflowed down her cheeks. Retelling the incident when she felt her life was going to end by a crazed madman sent fingers of fear up and down her body, despite the heat coming from Xavier's.

Seeing Selena cry was Xavier's undoing. Gathering her closer, he pulled her over his body, sandwiching her bare legs between his denim-covered ones. "Baby, don't. Please don't cry." His attempt to comfort and console her sounded weak, impotent, even to his own ears.

"I . . . I went to the police but they said they could . . . couldn't do anything because there were no witnesses." Sniffling, Selena pressed her face to the column of Xavier's strong neck, struggling to bring her emotions under control. "I'd thought about buying a gun, but changed my mind once I realized shooting or killing Derrick Perry wasn't worth me losing my freedom or my life. Someone at LAPD must have spoken to him, because the stalking stopped for a while. My agent was negotiating to renew my contract when Derrick showed up unexpectedly when I was leaving to go to the studio, this time with a handgun. He held it to his head, threatening to pull the trigger if I didn't tell him that I loved him, I would always love him and I couldn't live without him. If I refused, then he would kill me and then himself."

Gritting his teeth, Xavier swallowed an expletive. "The SOB probably was certifiably crazy."

"He was sick, Xavier."

"Sick or crazy he needed his ass kicked."

Selena smiled through her tears. "That sounds like something my brothers would say. I told him everything he wanted to hear, and then went back upstairs to my apartment where I called my agent and told him not to bother negotiating the contract because I was leaving L.A. I disconnected my phone, turned off my cell, packed up my clothes, sent a check to the landlord to cover the remaining months on my lease and left L.A. I drove cross-country, stopping whenever I saw a small town or city that looked interesting."

"Why didn't you go home?"

"That's probably the first place Derrick would've looked for me. I'd called my parents and lied about giving up acting. I told them I hated going to work in the dark and coming home in the dark, that a twelve- to fifteen-hour workday was beginning to take its toll on my physical and emotional well-being."

Cupping her hips, Xavier gently massaged the firm flesh under the cotton shorts. "Did they believe you?"

"I think so. It was my grandmother who didn't believe me. She made me promise to tell her everything once I got back to West Virginia. I stopped at a library in Topeka, Kansas, went online and spent hours researching the best towns and cities to live and visit. That's when I decided on Charleston. I'd already made up my mind to become a pastry chef, so finding a school was next on my agenda. Meanwhile, I'd called my dad to tell him I was coming home for Christmas.

"Grandma Lily came into my bedroom after everyone had gone to bed, gave me a look and I told her everything. She promised to keep my secret. However, she did tell Daddy that there had been an obsessed fan who'd discovered I'd come from Matewan and believed I was his wife in another lifetime. It was the first time I'd known my grandmother to lie. I reassured my family I was safe in Charleston because here I'm Selena Yates, not Raina Vaughn. I don't know if I was able to convince my father and brothers because whenever they pick me up at the airport they are armed to the teeth. And before you say it, no one here has ever asked if I was ever on television."

Xavier laughed, the sound rumbling his chest. "Don't tell me you can read minds?"

It was Selena's turn to laugh. "No, but Grandma Lily can. Folks call her a witch, but she's not bothered by it because she says it keeps them from messing with her."

Sobering, Xavier stared up at the lacy fabric. "Even though I hope he never happens, if Derrick Perry shows his face in Charleston, then he's in for a world of hurt."

"Please no, Xavier."

"The man threatened to kill you and you say 'please no.' If the men in your family are carrying guns, then they're not as confident or trusting as you are about your safety."

"My father is the sheriff."

"Are your brothers deputies?"

"No. Keith teaches high school math and Luke is an actuary."

"Two careers that don't require either of them to carry a licensed handgun. I think it's best Mr. Perry stay in L.A. because Charleston may prove hazardous to his health."

Selena struggled to free herself from Xavier's hold on her body. "Let me go, Xavier."

"Why? Because you don't want to face the possibility that your crazy-ass ex just might show up here? And what are you going to do? Pack up shop and run away again? There comes a time when you have to stop running, baby. You can't let some crazy person control your life when he's not able to control his own."

"I hear what you're saying."

"Listen to what I'm saying, Selena. I just want you to be careful."

"The shop is wired with direct access to the police and I never use the front door when I go upstairs."

Xavier loosened his firm grip on her body, shifting into a sitting position and bringing her up to straddle his thighs. He tunneled his hands through her hair, holding it off her face. "Have you thought about putting in a buzzer? That way everyone would have to be buzzed in and out."

"I have the bell."

He bit down on the back of his hand to keep from spewing invectives. "Please don't make me tell you what I think of *that* bell," he said between clenched teeth. "What if the bell rings and you're in the back? If you don't have the money for a buzzer —"

"It's not about money, Xavier," Selena countered.

"Then, what is it?"

A beat passed as she stared at Xavier staring back at her. His eyes were flat, cold and a muscle quivered at his jaw. He was angry, tension coming off him like storm-tossed waves pounding a beach. "I don't want to start and end my day thinking about someone coming after me."

His expression softened. "I just don't want to have to worry about you."

"And I'll make certain not to give you cause to worry about me. You're going to have to let me up, otherwise we're going to end up eating cardboard turkey."

Xavier didn't want to let her go. "If it burns, then I'll take you out to dinner."

"But I don't want to go out."

His eyebrows lifted. "You've told me what you don't want. What is it you want?"

Selena pondered the question. Could she afford to tell the man holding her protectively what lay in her heart? She decided if she and Xavier could have even a semblance of a normal relationship then she had to be truthful.

"I'm tired, Xavier. Tired of denying I'm a woman with physical needs and I'm sick and tired of blaming every man for the bastard who I'd allowed to turn my life upside down. My business is skyrocketing, while my personal life is in the toilet. You're the first man in two years I've allowed to kiss me, the first one to lie in this bed. I say all that because I know I'm more than ready for a one-night stand."

Xavier pressed kisses to her eyelids. "There's no way we're going to have a one-night stand. It's going to take at least six months for me to try and figure you out."

Selena stared at Xavier as if she'd never seen him before. "You think I'm difficult?"

"No. Not as difficult as you are an enigma. You run hot and cold when I least expect it, keeping me somewhat off balance. You appear to be acting even when you don't realize you are acting, Selena. What I want to know and figure out is who the real Selena

Yates is."

"There's nothing to figure out. What you see is what you get."

"And what is that?" he asked.

"A small-town girl who went to live in the big city, but left when she realized it wasn't for her. Living here suits my temperament — the weather, cuisine and laid-back life-style." A rumbling sound competed with their measured breathing. Selena froze. "Is that your belly?"

Xavier managed a sheepish expression. "Guilty as charged. I'd planned to prepare brunch for us, but somehow that was pre-empted because I couldn't keep my eyes open."

"What I can't understand is how you stayed up all night reading. Is the book that good?"

"It wasn't a book."

Selena gave him a skeptical look. "If it wasn't a book, then what is it?"

"I'll have to show you."

Now her curiosity was piqued. "What aren't you telling me, Xavier?"

"Come home with me."

The seconds ticked as they stared at each other, she seeing an open invitation in his eyes. It was an invitation she knew she would come to regret if she declined. "You know you're not right."

"Why am I not right?"

"If I don't find out what you were reading, then I'm not going to get any sleep. I'll go home with you, but if it's a collection of porn photos I'm going to hurt you real bad."

Xavier laughed, the sound bubbling from his chest and throat. "I can assure you it's not porn."

"Okay." He gave her the sensual smile she'd come to look for.

"If you want I'll make breakfast for you before I leave for work."

There came another pregnant pause. Xavier offering to make breakfast was his way of saying that he'd expected her to spend the night at his house. "You don't have to make breakfast, because I have to be here before eight." Monday was her banking day and she'd promised Lee that she would arrive at her house around ten.

"That's not a problem. I'll drop you off around seven-thirty."

She kissed his shoulder. "That sounds like a plan." Selena sat up, swinging her legs over the side of the bed. "I'll be in the kitchen."

Xavier watched her leave. It wasn't often that he'd found himself in a woman's bed and not made love to her. Again, he had to remind himself that Selena Yates was different. If she'd been any other woman who'd invited him in for coffee he would've taken her up on the offer; whether he would've wound up in her bed was another matter.

What he hadn't realized — until now — was within minutes of his walking into Sweet Persuasions he'd opened himself to allow Selena to see a part of him he'd always concealed from the women with whom he had been involved. She'd admitted to needing him, while he wanted her — all of her.

Chapter 8

"Don't you dare move," Xavier warned softly when Selena reached over to take his plate. "You cooked, so I'll clear the table."

"May I put away the leftovers?"

Xavier's eyes, brimming with tenderness and a passion that was becoming more and more difficult to conceal, stared at the woman whose cooking skills had exceeded his expectations. It was as if Selena Yates was a twenty-first-century renaissance woman. She was a fabulous cook, made delicious and eye-pleasing confectionery and the furnishings in her apartment had been selected with a discerning eye usually attributed to a professional decorator. It was as if she'd had cornered the monopoly on creativity.

Over a dinner of roast turkey with cornbread stuffing, baked sweet potatoes, smothered cabbage and light, fluffy biscuits, Selena told him about growing up in West

Virginia where who your people were meant everything. The Yates believed in God, family and country. They'd sacrificed their lives when they'd defended their country during the various wars and worked in coal mines, a few losing their lives in explosions and cave-ins. They were uncomplicated and very proud. Those who left because they'd yearned for a world beyond Matewan always returned to reconnect with their roots for holidays, weddings and funerals.

"Yes, baby. You may put away the leftovers."

Pushing back her chair, Selena stood up. She switched on the radio on the countertop, turning it to a station featuring soundtracks. "I can't believe I have to ask permission to move around my own kitchen," she mumbled under her breath.

"Now you know how I felt when you ordered me out of my own car," Xavier retorted, stacking plates and serving pieces.

"That was for your own good, Xavier Eaton."

"And my helping you clean up is for your own good, Selena Yates. You run a business that's open five days a week and you've posted a sign that all items are made on the premises. Should I assume that *you* make everything?"

She gave him a sidelong glance when he stood at the sink rinsing dishes before stacking them in the dishwasher. "I do."

"When do you get the time to do everything?"

"I do most of my baking on Mondays. I've learned not to make too many of any particular item because it will have to be thrown out. In my opinion, throwing away food is comparable to a mortal sin. Everything is made with natural ingredients, so they have a very short shelf life."

"Have you thought about donating what you consider leftovers to a food pantry or homeless shelter?"

Her hands stilled. "I hadn't thought of that."

Moving behind Selena, Xavier looped his arm around her waist. "I love this song. Come dance with me."

Turning in his loose embrace, Selena placed her left hand on Xavier's shoulder as he pulled her close. His low melodious voice singing "Hungry Eyes," from the *Dirty Dancing* movie soundtrack caressed her ear. She'd heard the song countless times, but this was the first time she actually listened to the lyrics.

As she melted into his strength, losing herself in the moment, music and the man,

Selena felt the anger, pain and fear she'd carried for longer than necessary evaporate like water on a hot griddle. When Xavier accused her of running hot and cold she hadn't had a comeback, because her emotions vacillated from liking to lust.

"Xavier!" His name came out in a strangled gasp when Selena felt the solid bulge under his jeans.

Lowering his head, Xavier buried his face in the loose waves framing Selena's face, struggling to keep from blurting out that she was special, very special from any other woman he'd met or known. He was thirty-four, a former career soldier who'd faced and cheated death; he hadn't died because he was destined to meet the woman cradled to his heart.

He felt closer to her than he had to those with whom he'd had long-term relationships. Why Selena Yates? She was younger and had come with emotional baggage, but that was inconsequential when compared to her other incredible qualities. He hadn't issued an idle threat when he told Selena about his plan for Derrick Perry if he showed up in Charleston. Perry would learn firsthand how it would feel to have a knife pressed to his throat or a gun thrust in his face.

Xavier's large hands slid down her back, cupping her hips and pulling her even closer. He'd stopped moving, singing. Their bodies molded from chest to thigh communicated without words. "Baby, please don't move."

Selena had heard the expression cat on a hot tin roof, and she knew what it meant. She was on fire — from head to toe — nerves screaming in sexual tension and frustration, the throbbing and moisture bathing her core and reminding her of how long it had been since she'd made love with a man. She did move. It was to anchor her arms under his shoulders, holding on to Xavier as if her next breath depended upon him for survival. The whimpers in the back of her throat slipped through her lips. She bit down on her lip as tremors shook her like a leaf in a strong wind.

The song ended, but for Xavier it had just begun. The lyrics echoed what he felt and had been feeling the first time Selena greeted him when he'd walked in Sweet Persuasions.

I've got hungry eyes. Each time he looked at Selena she had to have known that he wanted her.

I feel the magic between you and I. Whenever they occupied the same space he was aware of the sexual tension and sensuous light that burned brighter with each encounter. He'd met her four days ago when it seemed much longer. Although Selena had admitted he was the first man she'd allowed to kiss her or lie in her bed in two years, Xavier did not want to take advantage of her or her vulnerability.

Pressing his mouth to her ear, he whispered, "Why don't you pack what you need to stay over and I'll finish up here." He pulled back, meeting her wide-eyed gaze. "I want to assure you that nothing will happen that you don't want to happen."

Selena glanced up at Xavier, her heart hammering wildly in her chest. His gaze was hypnotic, mesmerizing. What spell had he cast over her wherein she wanted to sleep with a stranger? "Can you answer one question for me?"

His expression was impassive. "I'll try."

"What's happening between us? We met three days ago and —"

"It's been four days," Xavier interrupted with a wide grin.

"Okay, four. This is serious, Xavier." Her voice was soft, almost pleading.

"No, it's not, Selena. You want it to be serious, and I want us to have fun. I spent years in a war zone where I saw and did unspeakable acts. A year ago I lay in a military hospital not knowing whether I'd ever walk again, and if I did would it be with a prosthetic. So, please forgive me, but at this time in my life I don't do 'serious.' At least not very well," he added.

Selena recoiled as if someone had struck her. How had she been so caught up in her own angst that she hadn't considered what Xavier had gone through? Sleeping with him wasn't the issue, but the possibility of forming a relationship. After what she'd gone through with Derrick she feared commitment.

Her arms went up around his neck, pulling his head down. His warm, moist breath feathered over her mouth. "Will you remind me when I get too serious?"

Smiling, Xavier cradled Selena's face. He could feel her heart beating against his chest. It fluttered like a frightened bird's. "Yes."

Standing on tiptoe, she touched her lips to his. "There is something you should know about me. In high school I was known as the class clown. Whenever we had talent night I would always do stand-up."

"Were you X-rated or PG?"

"Xavier! Shame on you! Talent night was always held on school property. And, if my mama found out I was cussin' or telling dirty jokes in public it would've been all she wrote."

"Is your mama tough?"

"Whenever you go to Matewan I'll arrange for you to meet her and then you can judge for yourself." Selena kissed him again. "I'll be back as soon as I pack an overnight bag."

Selena didn't know what to expect when Xavier opened the door to his home, but it wasn't the spacious rooms, most of them empty, with exquisite parquet floors, tall narrow windows and second-story bedrooms with French doors opening onto spacious verandas. The wrought-iron gates protecting the Charleston single house and welcoming white porch were quintessential Charleston architecture.

Taking off her shoes and leaving them on a rush mat she wiggled her sock-covered toes. "Do you mind if I do a walkthrough — alone?"

Xavier looked at Selena, his expression mirroring confusion. He'd admitted to her that she was an enigma, but she was more than that. She was an ever-changing montage of emotions and appearances — a chameleon. It was no wonder people hadn't recognized her from her soap opera days.

"When I walk into a room not only do I want to see it, but I also need to feel it," she explained. "Homes are like people. They reflect one's personality." Selena rested her hands at her waist. "Why are you looking at me like that, Xavier?"

"How can an empty room have a personality?"

Selena didn't want to argue with him. "If you weren't so citified you'd know what I'm talking about."

He snorted. "And, you're not Miss Former L.A. Red Carpet?"

She flashed a sexy moue, drawing his gaze to linger on her lush mouth. "I'm a mountain girl down to the marrow in my bones." Her inflection was pure Appalachia.

Throwing back his head, Xavier let out a roar of unrestrained laughter. "Well, go on mountain girl. Do yo thang!"

"Sorry, boo, but you sound a little cheesy."

He sobered. "On that note, I think I'll go and make some coffee. Would you like some?"

"I prefer tea."

"How do you take your tea?"

"I like it with lemon and honey. If you don't have honey, then sugar."

Xavier headed toward the kitchen while

Selena climbed the staircase to the second floor. Hearing her speak in the dialect reminded him of a marine instructor assigned to the mountain warfare training center in Bridgeport, California. He'd also come from a mining town and had joined the corps to escape working in the mines as had generations of men in his family. Everyone called him Nails. Henry Withers was tall, lean *and* hard as nails. He'd earned a reputation as a guts-and-glory badass, but he had the uncanny ability to turn marines into men who were able to survive under the most extreme conditions.

The kitchen was the only room in the house Xavier didn't want changed. He'd relied on the contractor's recommendations when he'd chosen the cabinets and appliances. Top-of-the-line, eye-level ovens, warming drawers, dual dishwashers and side-by-side refrigerator/freezer were finished in burnished nickel to conceal fingerprints. The cooking island, with dual stainless-steel sinks, stovetop burners and grill and drawers for storage matched the off-white kitchen cabinets. The doors to the drawers and cabinets were magnetic, alleviating the need to choose hardware. A counter with a quartet of high stools was the perfect place to eat while watching a television built into a wall.

Xavier's morning routine was always the same: he got up, washed his face, brushed his teeth and then came downstairs to his workout room. Most days he logged two miles on the treadmill, lifted weights for fifteen minutes, then retreated to his en suite bath where he shaved and showered. He prepared breakfast and sat watching the morning news while he ate. It was on a rare occasion he would eat breakfast at school, where a resident chef prepared breakfast, lunch and dinner for the students, faculty and staff who lived on campus. Once he taught his last class, Xavier packed up and headed home.

The word was still strange to him because *home* had either been his parents' house, a campus, base or off-base military housing. And if he were truly honest with himself Xavier would admit that this was the first time in his life that he was completely independent. No more cafeterias, mess halls or officers' clubs. He could cook, thanks to the urging of Paulette Eaton; he could do laundry, separating light from dark colors; and he could iron, but had opted to send his shirts out. He could also clean — but again he had opted to contract with a cleaning service. His weekends were relegated to relaxing, not housecleaning, although all he had to do was dust the floors in the empty rooms.

Xavier stood at the French doors staring out at the garden with a trio of ancient oak trees draped in Spanish moss. The garden was the reason why he'd decided to purchase the house. After living in a region where he woke to see sand and an occasional olive tree, he'd wanted to look out on anything green, even if it was a tangle of weeds. The oak, palmetto and newly planted fruit trees would provide shade for generations while the garden would produce flowers year-round with annuals and perennials.

He felt rather than heard movement behind him and turned to find Selena walking into the kitchen. The fitted jeans clung to her hips and legs, long, smooth brown legs that turned him on.

"That was quick."

Selena sat on a stool, resting her elbows on the granite countertop and her chin on fisted hands. She stared at Xavier under lowered lids. "I saw all I needed to see."

Xavier closed the distance between them, leaning on the counter opposite her. "Well, what do you think?"

She saw the expectant look on his face, a look she'd seen on children when their parents contemplated buying them a new toy or video game. But the man leaning across the small space separating them was not a child, but someone with whom she'd committed to spend the night. Not only would she sleep under his roof but also in his bed. Xavier Eaton had purchased a house with four bedrooms but there was only one bed in the entire house, and it was in the master bedroom.

"You house is beautiful."

"And?" he asked lifting questioning eyebrows.

"And it has an amazing personality."

Xavier stood up straight. "What's with this personality business?"

"You saw my bedroom." He nodded. "If you didn't know me, what would you surmise from looking at the furnishings?"

Crossing his arms over his chest, Xavier gave Selena a long, penetrating stare. Suddenly he knew what she was talking about. "It's a woman's bedroom."

"What about that woman?"

"She's very feminine."

"What else, Xavier?"

"She's a little old-fashioned. The canopy bed, rocking chair and crocheted pieces are from another era. So is the ceiling fan. Even though many homes have ceiling fans, they are a throwback to days when there was no electricity. Then there's the quilt."

Satisfaction lit up Selena's eyes. "What about the quilt?" she asked.

"It's handmade and no doubt worth a great deal of money."

Her lips parted in a smile that reached her eyes. "Hey! My man knows his stuff!"

Hearing Selena call him "her man" sent a rush of pride racing through Xavier. He bowed gracefully from the waist. He wanted to be her man. He wanted to belong to her and she to him. Yet he knew intuitively that Selena was hesitant when it came to commitment. Unfortunately for him, her relationship with Derrick Perry had made her wary.

"Why thank you." He sobered. "Does this mean I pass the test?"

Selena nodded. "Yes. I'm all the things you said. Now, it's your turn. Judging from what you've shown me and the furnishings in your bedroom I'd say you are ultra-macho. The California-king mahogany bed with a padded-leather headboard screams masculinity. You like balance because you have two nightstands. Although you have more than enough closet space, you still have an armoire, chest, triple dresser and a padded-leather bench at the foot of the bed where you store books and magazines.

"You're a neat freak, Xavier Eaton, and you want everything in its own place. What you have to decide when you decorate the other bedrooms is whether they will be masculine, feminine or neutral-gender. You're a history buff, so I would suggest the sitting areas reflect a historical period that's either antebellum, Victorian or art deco with corresponding wall sconces. All of the bedrooms should have ceiling fans that complement the decor. The window shutters are in keeping with the overall architecture of the house, but if you want you can add sheers so when the shutters are open they will let light through while providing some privacy. Whatever you do, do not cover the floors — not even with area rugs."

"Is there anything else?"

"Are you a collector?"

Xavier smiled. "I have a collection of old maps, but they are reproductions."

"It doesn't matter, Xavier. If they're not framed, then get them framed."

"I have black-and-white photographs of different cities. I also have a collection of photos of players from the Negro Leagues."

Selena felt her mind working overtime. "The cityscapes can go in the various bedrooms, while the photos of the baseball players can be displayed in your home office." Xavier had set up a room adjacent to his workout space as an office. A workstation held a desktop, printer and other office equipment. The office was still a work in progress. Boxes labeled *Books* sat in a corner and built-in shelves were only half-filled with a collection on military history. "Have you thought about sweetgrass baskets? You can't live the low country and not own at least one basket."

"Don't they sell them down at the farmer's market?"

"Yes. You can also find weavers around the downtown area who will give you a better discount than what you'll find at the market. I saw one at the market that was selling for two thousand, but when I ran into a weaver on the street she sold me one that was similar for twelve hundred. Every once in a while she'll come into the shop to show me her inventory. I have a shelf in my workroom filled with them."

"Where would I put the baskets?"

"They would go nicely in the entryway on an antique drop-leaf table. I suggest putting up a rack where you can hang straw hats in various sizes, and replace the ceiling fixture with one that looks like a gaslight. Practically every room has a fireplace. Candles in different sizes would add a homey touch to the mantelpieces. There're antique shops on King Street where you should be able to pick up candelabras and chimneys to hold the candles."

Xavier came around the countertop, gently pulling Selena to her feet. "How did you come up with all of this so quickly?"

Selena told him about the dollhouse her grandfather had made for her and the number of years it took for her to decorate it. She also revealed how she'd wanted to become a decorator before she decided she preferred acting. "When most thirteen- and fourteen-year-old girls were reading teen magazines I read those that featured beautiful homes and gardens. Whenever my mama wanted me to help her in the kitchen I pretended I had to do homework when I was actually knitting or crocheting something to add to my dollhouse. Then she caught me. After that I had to do my homework at the kitchen table, and when I was finished, the cooking lessons followed. I hated having to watch a pot, but liked baking because once you put something in the oven you didn't have to check on it until it was done."

Xavier ran a finger down the length of her nose. "You still can become a decorator if you want."

Selena snorted delicately. "I don't think so. Most people have a plan A and B, but not a C."

Looping an arm around her waist, Xavier eased Selena to stand between his legs. "If you had a C what would it be?"

She gave his query a few seconds of thought. "Probably make Sweet Persuasions a mail-order business."

Xavier schooled his face not to reveal his surprise. He'd thought she would've said marriage and children. Most women he knew usually contemplated their future to include a husband and children. "Do you still want your tea?"

She smiled sweetly. "Yes. I also want to see what kept you up all night."

"It's upstairs. Why don't you go on up and get ready for bed and I'll bring you your tea in about twenty minutes."

Selena felt her heart lurch against her ribs before it seemingly sunk in her stomach and returned to her chest to form a knot, making breathing difficult. Xavier telling her to go upstairs and get into his bed brought everything into focus. She'd come with him to his home to discuss decorating and to see what had kept him from a restful night's sleep.

She'd made it known to him that she was willing to share her body, but now that it was to become a possibility she felt like a reticent virgin. But then, Xavier had promised that nothing would happen that she didn't want to happen.

Selena swallowed several times to moisten her constricted throat. "Make it half an hour. I always take a shower before I go to bed."

Xavier gave her bottom a light pat. "Take all the time you need."

Chapter 9

Selena lay in the middle of the bed, watching Xavier as he walked into the bedroom holding a steaming mug in each hand. Droplets of water glistened on his broad shoulders and on his bare chest. It was apparent that he had also showered. He wore a pair of drawstring cotton pajama bottoms that hung low on his slim hips.

As a chocolatier she had become an artist when it came to molding candy and desserts into various shapes. And at that moment, she wished she'd had pencil and paper so she could sketch the planes and hollows that sculpted Xavier Eaton's lean muscular body. The light from the table lamps cast shadows of orange and yellow over his brown skin. As he approached the bed, she noticed his face was several shades darker than his upper body.

"Which side do you sleep on?" she asked.

Xavier set the mugs down on glass coasters monogrammed with his initials. They were a gift from his sister. He smiled, thinking how young Selena looked with her hair pulled into a ponytail, and wearing a pajama top with tiny polka dots. He didn't know why, but he'd expected her to wear a lacy nightgown.

"Scoot over. I always sleep nearest the door." Waiting until Selena shifted to her left, he handed her the tea. Within seconds he was in bed, toasting her with his mug. *"Salute!"*

She smiled. "Cheers."

They sat in silence, sipping tea and coffee as if it were something they did every night. Xavier felt the peace and quiet that had evaded him from the moment his foot stepped onto Iraqi soil. Since age seven, he'd prepared himself for a life in the military. He'd studied and trained for combat. Yet when he saw the rifle flash of someone hiding in an abandoned building in Iraq, he suddenly realized he hadn't been prepared for the reality of war. Not until he'd returned fire did he finally believe that war was indeed hell.

If his experiences in Iraq and Afghanistan were hell, then sitting in bed with Selena Yates was as close to heaven as he could imagine. *Love is caring, sharing, giving and above all peaceful and quiet.* Right now he felt the impact of his father's words.

Xavier didn't know whether he was in love or falling in love with Selena because he didn't know what love was — at least not the kind of love other than for his family.

"Don't run away," he teased, as he sat on the side of the bed. Xavier walked toward the armoire across the room, opened it to reveal a flat-screen television and electronic components. He turned on the radio to a station featuring classical music. Beethoven's "Violin Concerto in D major op. 61" filled the bedroom. He lowered the volume with the remote until it was nothing more than background music. Xavier glanced over his shoulder at Selena. "Do you want me to change the station?"

Selena had settled back on the mound of pillows that cradled her head and shoulders, the scent of laundered linen wafting in her nose. "Please don't. It's very relaxing."

Xavier unlocked the wall safe, removed the key to the foot-locker and retrieved the pouch with the journals. He got into bed with her, turning the lamp on his bedside table to the highest setting. Slipping on the cotton gloves, he removed the journal from the pouch and placed the one with the earliest entries on Selena's lap. His eyes met her questioning gaze as he opened the tattered cover.

Selena read the faded writing on the first page. "Is this authentic?" She couldn't disguise the awe in her voice.

"I believe it is. I'm not an expert, but I was able to verify many of the facts."

She stared at Xavier. "Where did you get these?"

He told her how he'd come into possession of the journals. "After I finish reading them, I'm going to the courthouse to check the census, birth and death records. Hopefully some of Josiah Chadburn's descendants still live in Charleston."

"What if they do?"

"Then they're going to get an unexpected gift."

Selena shifted again, settling her head against the pillows, her shoulder and leg touching Xavier's. "Now I see why you were up all night reading."

Xavier returned Josiah's diary to the pouch, leaving the journal and the gloves on the bench at the foot of the bed. "Reading it is slow going. Not only do I take notes, but I stop to verify certain facts online."

Selena turned off the lamp on her side of the bed, and went completely still. She couldn't move, not with Xavier's chest pressed to her back. She giggled like a little girl when he nuzzled the side of her neck. "What are you doing?"

"Sniffing you," he mumbled. "You smell delicious."

She shifted to face him, catching and holding her breath in the diffused light. Xavier had dimmed his bedside lamp and the stubble on his jaw only enhanced his rugged handsomeness. He moved closer without moving, as she closed her eyes. His warm breath seared her face seconds before he claimed her mouth with a restrained yet savage intensity. The sexual tension that had begun what now seemed eons ago had reached a point where it had to be resolved.

"Are you all right?" he whispered against her parted lips.

Selena nodded, smiling. "I'm good."

She wanted to tell Xavier she was more than good — that she felt incredibly whole being with him. They hadn't made love, yet she felt as complete as if she would've had an orgasm. It was that feeling of peaceful renewal. Selena knew Xavier would be shocked if he knew her initial attraction to him was purely sexual. When he'd walked into Sweet Persuasions for the first time she'd been hard-pressed not to gawk at him.

He wasn't a truffle, torte or mousse, but the entire patisserie array to be devoured until sated.

Her reaction to him was like a pot of water under a low flame, simmering then boiling over. When he'd put his hand on her thigh at Ma Bell's, she'd warmed to his touch. The heat simmered when they'd lain in her bed together and almost boiled when they'd danced together. Now that she lay in his bed, Selena knew their fragile relationship had to be resolved and the sexual tension assuaged.

She told him that her attraction to Derrick had been immediate. What she didn't tell him was that it hadn't been physical but it was intellectual. He was well traveled and intelligent. There wasn't any topic he hadn't been able to discuss. She would tease him about trying out for *Jeopardy,* but he'd said he would probably freeze up and not be able to phrase the answer in the form of a question.

They dated for two months before going to bed together. Derrick was as inept in bed as he was brilliant out of bed. Each time they'd tried to make love, he'd become a bumbling partner. And after a while Selena stopped him before he could begin. Their relationship had begun as friendship and she was content for it to remain that way.

Her sexual experience had been limited to one man before she'd met Derrick. She'd almost lost her virginity to a fellow drama student. But when she told him it was to be her first time, he ran in the opposite direction claiming he was out to have fun, not get involved with a needy woman who'd given him her virginity.

The first and only sexual encounter had been with a screenwriter, a much older and very experienced man. He had no qualm about taking her virginity and was completely uninhibited. He taught her to love her body and what to do to bring herself and her partner ultimate satisfaction. Their brief liaison ended when he remarried one of his three ex-wives.

She put her left leg over his thigh. "Am I hurting you?" There had been times when Xavier thought she hadn't noticed that he limped slightly, favoring his right leg.

"No," Xavier said truthfully. His hand searched under the hem of her pajamas, his fingers caressing her smooth legs. "Do you shave your legs?"

"No. I have them waxed."

His eyebrows lifted a fraction. "Doesn't that hurt?"

"A little. It takes some getting used to."

Xavier grunted. “That’s something I don’t want to get used to.”

Selena traced his eyebrow with her finger. “Some men get their eyebrows waxed.”

“Hell no! None of that metrosexual crap for me.”

Her hand went to his jaw. The stubble of his chin felt good under her palm. “I thought you were a badass, Xavier.”

He smiled. “I am, but that doesn’t include putting hot wax on my body, then ripping off hair *and* flesh.”

“Your eyebrows are nice, but there are a few stray strands I could tweeze.”

“No tweezing and no waxing.”

“But —”

Xavier’s mouth covered hers, aborting her protest. Everything changed when his hands probed under her pajama top, massaging the tight flesh over her ribs, her breath coming in quick gasps from pleasure radiating from her chest downward. Enraptured by her own burning desires and awakened passion, Selena’s hands moved over his chest to his flat belly.

“Touch me, baby!” Xavier gasped.

Reaching between his thighs, she caressed his hardened sex through the cotton fabric. The heat from his shaft warmed her hand. Her fingers went to the drawstring, untying it as Xavier raised his hips to help ease out of the pajama bottoms. In less than a minute her pajamas joined his at the foot of the bed.

Selena lay on her back, staring up at her soon-to-be lover hovering over her. Their eyes met, they shared a knowing smile. It was about to begin, the sensual dance of desire that would cease to separate them if only for a few minutes.

Xavier cupped a firm breast, squeezing it gently. "You are so perfect," he whispered. Everything about Selena was natural from her beautiful face, healthy hair, flawless skin, firm breasts perched high above a narrow ribcage, the flair of her womanly hips and long, slender, shapely legs and feet. His thumb grazed her nipple until it hardened, the areola pebbling under his palm.

Selena closed her eyes rather than stare at the length of throbbing flesh between Xavier's muscular thighs. Her breathing quickened, coming in short gasps. Sensations she'd forgotten came alive. Liquid fire rippled through her veins as a rush of sexual awareness held her captive.

Xavier lowered his head, his mouth searching for Selena's, and she returned his kiss. His tongue plunged into her mouth at the same time he tunneled his fingers through her hair. The elastic band that had secured her ponytail lay on the pillow as he gently massaged her scalp.

He'd become a sculptor, beginning with her hair and working his way down to her toes. Tongue and teeth explored her earlobe, column and base of her neck and throat before he fastened his mouth to her breast, eliciting a keening from Selena that made the hair rise on the back of his neck. The magnitude to which she responded to him was shocking and, as he aroused her, his own passion grew hotter, stronger, fearing he would ejaculate before penetrating Selena.

Sitting back on his knees, he leaned over and opened the drawer in the nightstand, taking out a condom from the supply he kept there. His gaze met and fused with Selena's as he opened the packet, withdrew the circle of latex and rolled it down the length of his tumescence. She'd admitted he was the first man in her bed since she'd moved to Charleston, and she was the first woman in his since he'd returned to live in Charleston. It had taken less than a week for him to make up his mind that he wanted her to be the last.

He would turn thirty-five in April, he'd served his country under the most extreme conditions, dated a lot of women, slept with some, but none had intrigued him the way Selena did. Like a large cat he sniffed her neatly cut furred mound, inhaling her body's natural fragrance mingling with the scent of her rising desire. Xavier wanted the woman in his bed, wanted to be inside her, but wanted to bring Selena to climax before he released his own passion. Alternating kissing her inner thighs with flicking his tongue over and pulling her clitoris gently between his teeth he felt the changes going on in Selena's body.

Selena felt as if millions of tiny furry creatures were crawling over, in and out of her body. Her nerves were screaming and her heart pounded painfully against her ribs. *Why is he torturing me?* she thought. "Please, Xavier. Love me." She pleaded with him over and over. It becoming a litany.

Xavier heard her pleas but he wasn't ready to make love to her. His thumb replaced his tongue when he massaged the swollen button of flesh at the apex to her vagina. She screamed; the sound echoed, lingering in the room. She screamed again, this one followed by a rush of moisture on his fingers. It was as if he'd held his hand under a leaky faucet. Sliding up the bed, he guided his erection between Selena's legs and his tongue into her mouth.

Selena gasped, this time when she felt the probing assault on her celibate flesh. She bit on her lip as the pressure increased with each inch of Xavier's erection disappearing inside her body. This time her pleas were silent. She couldn't wait for the pain to stop. It was as if she were a virgin again. Her fingers went from gripping the sheet to her fingernails making half-moon impressions on Xavier's back.

He began to move, pushing and pulling, thrusting and withdrawing. The pain and burning disappeared, replaced by unadulterated pleasure. Everything about Xavier Eaton was magnified: the power in his incredibly fit body, the now familiar smell of him she could detect in a darkened room crowded with men.

Xavier felt as close to death as he would come without actually dying. The wet flesh sheathing his blood-engorged sex opened and closed, each time squeezing him tighter, harder. "You feel so good. You are so beautiful," he whispered in her ear, over and over until it had become his litany.

Selena felt like crying. Xavier wasn't only making love *to* her — he was making love *with* her. Lifting her hips, she met him, establishing a rhythm that took her beyond herself. *No, no, no!* the voice in her head screamed. What they were sharing was lust not love. And she didn't want to believe she was falling in love with a man she hadn't known a week.

Xavier felt as if he'd run a grueling race.

Her mind was flitting in every direction and she didn't want to think about falling in love or being in love. She knew she'd tried thinking of any and everything because she wanted to hold off climaxing as long as possible. Once she experienced an orgasm it would be over and selfishly she never wanted it to be over.

Xavier slowed, his rigid sex moving in and out of her body. Then he changed the cadence, quickening and thrusting strongly. Each time she felt an orgasm seize her he changed rhythm, leaving her in limbo. She wanted to climax but she also didn't want the pleasure to end.

The whimpers in the back of her throat escaped, she writhing and moaning shamelessly. Then, without warning, the first orgasm exploded, followed by another and then another, shattering her into infinite pieces of ecstasy. Chills, then heat swept over her with the unrestrained growl that accompanied Xavier's release. Babbling unintelligently, he collapsed heavily on her languid body.

At first Selena welcomed his weight and the feel of his ebbing sex inside her. But Xavier had become dead weight where she could hardly breathe. "Xavier."

"Hmm."

"You have to get off me, because I can't breathe."

Xavier did not want to move. Being inside the softness of her moist heat made him feel connected to Selena. He rolled over, lying on his back and waiting for his breathing to return to a normal rate. Reaching for her hand, he laced their fingers together. There was no need to talk — everything they needed to say had been said. Their bodies had done the talking.

Selena's fingers went limp, and when he turned to look at her he saw that she'd fallen asleep. Untangling their fingers, Xavier slipped out of bed and walked in the direction of the en suite bath to discard the condom. When he returned he found Selena had shifted position. She lay on her side, the sheet pulled up over her breasts. He got into bed, picked up the remote device and turned off the radio, flicked off the lamp and slid down so the pile of pillows cradled his head and shoulders.

Xavier wondered what it was about the

woman in his bed that made him want to take care of her when it was obvious she could take care of herself. Selena had proven that when as an eighteen-year-old she'd left her hometown of less than a thousand to travel three thousand miles to California.

She'd graduated college, realized her dream to become an actress and the only blip on her personal radar was Derrick Perry. She'd left L.A. to start over in a new city and with a new career. Although Selena was the embodiment of an independent, strong, black woman Xavier couldn't rid himself of the need to protect her.

Lowering his arms, he turned and pulled Selena closer until her back was pressed to his chest. There was only the sound of measured breathing when he finally joined her in sleep.

Selena felt a draft when the door to the shower stall opened and Xavier stepped inside. "What are you doing?" Dots of shaving cream clung to his chin.

Xavier winked at Selena. She'd covered her hair with a plastic shower cap. "I'm trying to go green and save water."

Her smile was dazzling. "When did you become an environmentalist?"

"Three seconds ago." He took the bath sponge covered with scented gel from her. "Turn around, sweetheart, so I can wash your back."

Selena complied, presenting Xavier with her back. He'd gotten up earlier, leaving her sleeping soundly, completed his two miles on the treadmill and a twenty-minute weights workout. He'd used the half bath off the kitchen to shave because he hadn't wanted to wake Selena. However, during his absence she'd gotten up and made up the bed.

"Hey! That's not my back." Xavier had started at the nape of her neck, working his way down her spine and lingering at the small of her back. He'd given her a start when he reached between her legs.

Bracing his hands on the wall over her head, Xavier moved closer. "Sorry about that."

Selena stared at the large hands with the long tapered fingers and square-cut nails. "Why don't I believe you?" she asked, when he fastened his mouth to the side of her neck.

"I don't know."

She turned, coming face-to-face with the man who'd made exquisite love to her. Going on tiptoe, she looped her arms around his neck as water from a large showerhead beat down on their naked bodies and pulled his head down. “Good morning,” she breathed into his open mouth, her mint-flavored breath mingling with his. Then she did what Xavier had done to her the night before.

Her mouth charted a path from his mouth, the side of his strong neck and chest; she lingered to suckle his breasts, giggling when his flat nipples plumped from her oral assault. She sank to her knees as her rapacious mouth continued its downward journey. With one hand braced on his flat belly, she grasped his semierect penis. Selena didn’t give him a chance to react when she took him into her mouth.

Xavier bellowed as if he’d been branded by a hot iron. He tried pulling out, but she clamped her teeth on his rigid flesh. The pressure was not enough to cause him pain, yet he didn’t want to risk forcing her head away. It would take some very creative explaining to his doctor as to how he wound up with scrapes and teeth marks on his package.

His chest rose and fell heavily. His hands fisted and he gave into the delicious sensations while praying his knees wouldn’t give way. She pulled back to catch her breath, giving Xavier the advantage when he reached under her arms and pulled her to stand. Cupping her bottom, he lifted her effortlessly, anchoring her legs around his waist.

Selena panicked. "You can't go inside me without protection!"

"I'm not." Those were the last two words Xavier said as he concentrated on bringing them both to completion. He managed to hold on to Selena with one arm while he reached between his legs, positioning his erection between their bodies and then spreading her legs wider, and rubbed his blood-engorged sex against her vagina.

Selena had heard of dry humping, but they were far from dry. She'd gone down on Xavier and he'd turned the tables. He hadn't penetrated her yet the pleasure was as intense as if he had. Waves of ecstasy throbbed through her, the pleasure explosive as Xavier moved his penis against the folds of her vagina and clitoris. Gasping in sweet agony, she cried, her tears mingling with the water beating down on her head and body. The raw sensuousness of the act overrode everything she'd ever experienced.

Bracing his back against the wall, Xavier couldn't pull his gaze away from Selena's breasts. They were like ripened fruit swaying gently with the wind. A moan slipped through her quivering lips, followed by keening that was his undoing.

Holding her flush against his throbbing sex, he went completely still; closing his eyes as he spilled his passion in the shower. Somewhere between sanity and madness, he felt Selena shaking uncontrollably, her breath coming in lingering moans of surrender.

Resting her head on her lover's shoulder, Selena pressed a kiss there. "You are a very bad boy, Xavier Eaton."

"Sorry, but you're the bad one. Keep it up and I'll recommend you stay after school for detention."

Selena laughed. "Will you be my teacher?"

Pulling back, Xavier gave her a gentle look. "Of course. There's no way I would trust you around another teacher."

"Why not?"

A beat passed. "You just might corrupt the poor man."

Selena laughed, then sobered. "Xavier?"

"What is it?"

"The water is getting cold."

He ran a finger down her nose. "Haven't you ever taken a cold shower?"

"No. And I don't want to."

This time they managed to shower before

the water had become ice cold. Selena dried off, applied a scented body crème and stepped into a set of underwear. A pair of tan cropped pants, a long-sleeved black T-shirt and black-leather mules completed her casual look. She went into the bathroom to style her hair and when she emerged Xavier was dressed in a crisp white shirt, blue tie and navy-blue slacks with a red stripe along the side going from waist to hem. A jacket with a name tag and medals indicating his rank lay across the bed. Although Xavier wasn't active military he was still military. The cropped haircut, highly polished shoes and ramrod-straight posture were certain clues.

"I love a man in a uniform," she whispered when he led her out of the house to his car.

Xavier wanted Selena to love the man, not the uniform. After their unbridled coupling in the shower his emotional wellbeing had short-circuited. He never would've expected her to be that spontaneous *and* uninhibited. He'd told her he wanted spontaneity and she'd given him that and more. So much more than he could've imagined.

He assisted her into the car, then came around and hung his uniform jacket on a hook behind the front seat. Sliding into the Porsche, he started it up and stared through the windshield. "I want you to select the furniture for the house."

Selena watched the hand on Xavier's watch make a full revolution. "You want me to pick out the furniture?" He nodded. "You trust my taste?"

Resting his arm over the back of her seat, he turned to meet her eyes. "I trust *you.*"

"What if I go online and select what I think you would like. Then you can give me your opinion. I'll also look for a furniture company that can deliver in a reasonable amount of time."

"I don't want to wait six months for a dining room table," Xavier said.

"I'll probably use the company where I bought my furniture. They deliver in two to three days along the east coast."

He tugged playfully at her ponytail. "That sounds good."

Selena settled back in her seat as Xavier drove out of the driveway, waiting for an opening before maneuvering into the flow of Monday morning rush-hour traffic. "Do you intend to paint your walls?" Every wall in the house was covered with primer.

"Yes. I wanted to wait until the rooms were furnished before deciding on what color the walls should be." He gave her a quick glance. "Why did you ask?"

"Just curious."

He smiled. "Are you talking about a room's personality?"

Selena scrunched up her nose. "You're a quick learner."

Resting his hand on her thigh, Xavier gave it a gentle squeeze. "I have a good teacher."

He dropped her off along the street at the rear of her apartment building, waiting until she disappeared before driving away. Images of what he'd shared with Selena Yates stayed with him throughout the day. They hadn't talked about whether they would see each other before the cookout at the Mayers', but Xavier knew he had to be careful not to make the same mistake as Derrick Perry. He would give her the space she claimed she needed, and whenever they did come together it would make the encounter even more profound — at least it would be for him.

CHAPTER 10

Selena drove into the driveway of the house belonging to Douglas and Leandra Mayer. Sandhurst, a quiet community, was close to the city, yet far enough away from Charleston's hustle and bustle. Lovely brick homes, graced by live oaks and lush lawns provided the ideal setting for comfortable family living. The front door opened and Leandra waved to her. She wore a man's shirt over a pair of cuffed jeans. A wide headband held loose curls off her face.

Selena got out of her minivan and approached her, the two women exchanging air kisses. "You look wonderful."

Leandra rested a hand over her belly. "Thank you. I feel good. Please come in."

She followed her through a spacious foyer, living room with contemporary furnishings and into a large eat-in modern kitchen. Opening her leather tote, Selena took out a small white box tied with blue and white polka-dot ribbon, handing it to her host.

"You didn't have to bring anything."

Selena angled her head. "I was raised never to show up at someone's house empty-handed."

"So was I, but I truly don't need anything sweet because once I open this box I'll probably inhale everything in one sitting."

"There are only about a dozen assorted butter cookies and a few pieces of fudge."

Leandra placed the box on the countertop next a coffeemaker. "Even though I've given up coffee, I'll have one or two with a glass of milk."

"You have a very nice house," Selena complimented, glancing around the kitchen.

"Thank you. I'll give you a tour after we eat." Leandra gestured to a chair at the table under a skylight. She'd set the table for two. "We moved in right after the new year and I'm still decorating it. I hope you like shrimp and grits."

Selena had noticed the other night that Leandra jumped from topic to topic without pausing to take a breath. "I love them."

"Good. Have you eaten them at the Charleston Place Hotel?"

"No. Why?"

Leandra flashed a Cheshire-cat grin. "After a lot of trial and error I managed to duplicate the recipe. I didn't realize I had to use stone-ground grits instead of the regular hominy." She kissed her fingertips. "It's to die for."

"Do you need help with anything?"

"No. Just sit and relax. I have everything under control. The grits are cooked so I just have to make the shrimp sauce."

She sat watching Leandra as she moved around the kitchen with black appliances, white cabinetry and a black-and-white vinyl floor. She stared at the images on a muted television positioned under a cabinet.

Leandra opened the refrigerator and removed a bowl of large, deveined shrimp. "I hope you weren't upset with me Friday when I said that I'd had a crush on Xavier."

Selena sat stunned, temporarily mute. She'd hoped Leandra hadn't invited her to her home to talk about Xavier. "Of course I wasn't upset," she said, recovering her voice. "That was a long time ago."

"That it was, but it was a source of contention between me and Doug for a long time. That's why it took so long for us to make it official."

"I don't understand."

Leandra poured enough olive oil into an iron skillet to coat the bottom, waiting for it to heat before adding the shrimp, which she'd sprinkled with salt and pepper. "Doug and I were dating for about a year when one of my girlfriends who knew that I'd really liked Xavier let it slip to Doug that he was no more than a stand-in for his friend."

Selena frowned. "That's so mean."

"She was a real bitch. I later found out that she liked Doug but he wouldn't give her the time of day."

"How long did you and Doug date before you were finally married?"

"Ten years. We dated, broke up and saw other people, then started the crazy cycle all over again. Doug thought I was still carrying a torch for Xavier, and I got tired of trying to convince him that I had gotten over him. I met a guy who is a curator at a museum in Columbia and when word got back to Doug that I was thinking of relocating to Columbia he got his act together."

"Were you seriously thinking of relocating?"

Leandra smiled at Selena over her shoulder. "You're damn skippy I was. Doug thought I was moving to be with a man when in reality it was to accept a position with the museum. Ian and I are friends, and if I'd accepted the position with the museum he would've been my boss. And you know what they say about taking a crap where you eat."

"I hear you," Selena intoned.

Fortunately she'd never been faced with that situation, but she would've preferred it to what she'd gone through with Derrick. She was still thinking about Xavier's suggestion that she go to a buzzer system. Her customers were used to turning the knob and walking into Sweet Persuasions, and she wondered if installing a buzzer would impact her business.

"How did you meet Xavier?"

"He was a customer."

Leandra laughed. "How convenient. All you have to do is stand there and then decide who you'd like to date."

Selena wasn't about to tell her host how she'd come to go out with Xavier in the first place. And there was no way she was going to tell her that they'd slept together four days later. They were consenting adults and it was no one's concern what they did behind closed doors.

"A few men have come into the shop, but he was the only one that I'd found myself attracted to."

The kitchen was filled with mouthwatering smells when Leandra sautéed garlic and shallots in the pan. "That's because he is gorgeous. He's like fine wine. He gets better with age. He was quite the ladies' man when he was at The Citadel. Girls from the other colleges were always throwing their panties at him, but Xavier seemed oblivious to all the attention. That's why I liked him. He wasn't a dog like some guys that tried to see how many girls they could sleep with before graduating."

"Are you sure I can't help with anything?" Selena asked.

She didn't want to discuss Xavier with Leandra. It wasn't as if they were engaged and she needed to know everything about the man she'd planned to marry. And, even if she were to marry, there were some things she didn't need to know about a man. There were women who demanded a man tell them about every woman he'd slept with. Her mantra was what you don't know can't hurt you.

Leandra gestured to the coffeemaker. "If you want, you can brew a pot of coffee."

Selena preferred tea to coffee, but today she would have a cup. Pushing off the chair, she opened the canister with a *C* and measured enough grounds into the basket for two cups. By the time the distinctive aroma of brewing coffee filled the kitchen Leandra had ladled grits into a deep bowl, adding a topping of shrimp, garlic, shallots, diced yellow tomato, fresh minced basil and fresh lemon zest.

"I hope you aren't lactose intolerant because I added heavy cream. The only thing I left out is the white wine. I didn't add salt, because I have to watch my sodium intake."

Selena took the bowls from Leandra and carried them to the table. "Ohmigosh! This smells incredible."

"I have it at least twice a week, and it's a wonder I'm not big as a blimp."

Selena filled a cup with coffee while Leandra poured milk into a glass from a bottle in the refrigerator. They returned to the table and on cue bowed their heads to bless their food, then picked up spoons and began eating.

It wasn't the first time she'd eaten shrimp and grits, but when her mother made the dish she'd usually add cheese, andouille sausage and Cajun seasoning. "Eating this several times a week can really make you thick," she said after taking a sip of coffee.

Leandra nodded. "There's nothing like Southern cooking."

"Are you originally from the South?"

"No. I was born and raised in New Jersey. I came South to go to college and stayed."

"So your little baby will grow up saying 'ya'll' and 'yes, ma'am'."

"I know you're from down here, but it took me a long time to figure out certain words. Doug, who is from Tennessee, has had to translate from time to time." A frown found its way across Leandra's features. "What I couldn't understand was that Doug's folks weren't upset that he was marrying a black girl, but that I was from up North. Go figure."

"Folks are still biased about where you come from. It wasn't so bad for me when I lived in California because it's a state that's home to so many ethnic groups. But during my high school class trip to New York people would turn around stare at us as if we'd come from space once we opened our mouths."

"It's hard to detect your Southern drawl."

She didn't have a drawl because she'd worked with a speech coach. She never would've gotten work as an actress if people couldn't understand what she was saying. Even foreign actors were able to mimick a Midwest inflection if they were competing for roles that called for them to be American.

"I worked hard to get rid of it."

"Why did you do that?"

"When you operate your own business and you have to talk to people in different parts of the country you want to sound more nonspecific than regional." It wasn't a complete untruth. As it was, some telephone customers had asked her to repeat certain words because they hadn't understood her.

Smiling, Leandra closed her eyes briefly. "I'm glad you came because you've saved me from losing my mind. I get up to see Doug off, then go back to bed. I get up again when I feel hungry, then spend the rest of the day cleaning rooms that don't need to be cleaned, watch TV, eat again, etcetera, etcetera, etcetera until Doug comes home."

This confirmed for Selena that Leandra *was* bored and lonely. She was on leave from her teaching position and because she and Douglas were newcomers to Sandhurst she probably hadn't befriended anyone in the middle-class community of young professionals.

"Treasure doing nothing because once you become a mother your life as you know it will never be the same."

"You sound like my mother-in-law."

"I don't know your mother-in-law, but she's right. My sister-in-law is also pregnant and she has what she calls a 'pregnant bucket list' — things she must do before the babies come."

"Did you say 'babies'?"

"Yep. She's carrying twins."

Leandra pressed her hands together in a prayerful gesture. "When I found out I was pregnant I prayed I'd have a healthy baby, and then I prayed for twins. As they say back in Jersey — 'ba-da bing, ba-da boom.' I would've had my two babies and that's all she wrote."

Selena could not help laughing. Leandra had a wonderful sense of humor. "You're still young enough to have another child."

"I don't know if I'm willing to risk getting pregnant again. I went through four months of nausea morning, noon and night. If, and I do mean *if,* I decide I want another baby, then someone other than *moi* will carry it."

"Don't tell me you're thinking about a surrogate mother?"

"You're damn skippy. I was so sick that instead of gaining weight I had begun to lose it. Not funny. Right now I'm at my normal weight. If it wasn't for the belly you'd never know I was carrying a baby."

"It will all be worth it once you see your baby for the first time."

Leandra exhaled a contented sigh. "I know. It's just getting there that bothers me.

Doug says he's going to be in the delivery room videotaping. I told him if that tape goes viral he's done."

Selena's mouth dropped open. "He's going to upload it to the internet?"

"He claims he'd never do that. But you know how things mysteriously pop up in cyberspace."

"No comment."

She did not want to imagine someone uploading footage on her in a compromising situation. It was why she'd never slept with any of the actors she dated. One had willingly become embroiled in an incident where he was videotaped in a lewd and licentious situation that boosted rather than damaged his career.

Leandra touched a napkin to her mouth. "I know you told me you can't stay long, so let me show you the house. We'll start upstairs and work our way down."

Pushing off the chair, Selena walked with Leandra up a back staircase to the second floor. Doug's wife had decorated her home reminiscent of an art gallery. The walls were oyster-white, the bedrooms spare — almost spartan in appearance. *Simplicity* and *austere* were the adjectives that came to mind. Framed paintings and prints were the focal point in all the rooms.

Leandra opened the door to a room connecting it with the master bedroom. "This will be the baby's room."

The proposed nursery was a dramatic departure from the other spaces. Painted a pale butter-yellow with a border of farm and zoo animals on a background of kiwi-green, the room was warm, inviting. A green-and-yellow shaggy area rug covered most of the bleached-pine plank flooring.

"Very, very nice," Selena crooned. Aside from a white-wicker rocking chair with a matching footstool, the room claimed no other furniture. A pile of knitted and crocheted crib blankets were stacked on the rocker's seat cushion.

"I still have to buy furniture and decide on what I want on the walls."

"Did you knit these?" Selena ran her fingertips over a blanket with a chevron pattern.

Leandra walked over to a closet and opened the door. "Come take a look."

Selena peered into a large canvas storage unit filled with plastic bags containing booties, sweaters and hats. Leandra had mentioned when they were at Ma Bell's about knitting, but she had to have knitted during every waking minute to produce what filled the bin.

"You have enough here to go into business selling homemade baby clothes."

"That's what Doug has been telling me."

"He's right, Lee."

Crossing her arms under her breasts, Leandra angled her head. "I still haven't decided whether I'm going back to teaching or staying home with my baby. If I do stay home, then going into business is something that's doable. I wouldn't have to hire a nanny or leave my baby at a day care center."

"Whatever you decide, I want to be your first customer. I'd like to buy a couple of crib blankets, sweaters and booties. That will give me more time to piece several quilts for my niece or nephew."

"You quilt?"

Selena nodded. "Yes. My grandmother taught me."

"Hand or machine?"

"I prefer to hand quilt." She took a surreptitious glance at her watch. "Can we talk about this next week?" Selena knew if she didn't get back to the shop she would be forced to work late into the night. She liked running her own business because she didn't have to deal with a boss or supervisor, could set her own hours and had the option of accepting or refusing an order.

There were days when she cursed Derrick for forcing her to leave L.A., and there were times when she wanted to thank him for forcing her to recognize and develop what was a natural talent.

She was an artist with a discerning eye for detail and harmonious color. A brownie was a brownie until she added butterscotch chips, caramel or chocolate syrup and made ordinary extraordinary.

Leandra hugged Selena. "Of course. I know that you're really busy, but thank you for hanging out with this hormonal preggo."

"Thank you for the grits and shrimp. We'll definitely have to do it again. I'll let you know when I have a down week and we'll go shopping."

They retraced their steps, Leandra standing in the doorway waving as Selena backed out of the driveway. She was still in the same position when the mail carrier walked up the path with a stack of magazines. Selena suggesting she sell handmade baby knits was something worth thinking about. She took the mail, then walked into the house, closing the door behind her.

Selena's hands stopped dipping and coating tempered chocolate with cocoa powder, coconut and nuts spread out on parchment paper when the shop phone rang. Her head popped up and she stared at the display. She'd made it a habit not to answer the telephone when Sweet Persuasions was closed for business. Wiping her hands on a towel, she reached for the receiver when she saw the name on the caller ID.

"Hello." It had been five days since she'd seen or spoken to Xavier, but they had communicated by email.

"Hello to you, too. I called your apartment, but when I didn't get an answer I figured you'd be in the shop."

Her stomach did a little flip-flop when she heard his voice. "I would be at home but I got a call earlier this morning for truffles." Xavier's deep rich chuckle caressed her ear.

"Yum, yum. I'm calling because I like what you've selected for the bedrooms. But are you sure you want to order twin beds for the smaller room?"

Selena had spent hours going through pictures of bed, dining and living room furniture on a popular furniture website. After she'd chosen the items for each room, she'd attached them in an email to him.

"I'm very sure, Xavier. What if you have houseguests who don't want to share a bed?" She'd recommended queen-size beds for the other two bedrooms.

"I hadn't thought about that. I'll go along with whatever you want."

Anchoring the receiver between her chin and shoulder, Selena went back to dipping the ganache in chocolate, coating them in the mixture, then setting them on a wire rack to let excess chocolate drip off. "It's not about what I want," she countered. "It's your house, so the final decision rests with you." Silence came through the earpiece. "Xavier, are you there?"

"Yes, I'm here. I was checking the weekend movie listings. If you're not busy tomorrow night I'd like to take you to dinner and a movie."

Selena was going to tease him about asking her out for a date, but there was something in his voice that made her feel slightly uncomfortable. It had been a week since they'd gone to Ma Bell's for date night and two days later they were in bed together.

Had he felt that she'd used him for sex? Or had she been too uninhibited in the shower? A lot of men would have been blowing up her phone asking to see her again, but not Xavier. Their emails were generic with no declarations of affection. He'd begun his emails to her with "Dear Selena" and ended with "XPE." At first she'd thought him a little too formal, then dismissed it because if someone hacked into his email account there wouldn't be any incriminating correspondence.

"Dinner and a movie sound nice."

"Where would you like to eat, and is there a particular film you'd like to see?"

Selena smiled. He was giving her the option of choosing where they would go. "No. I'll let you pick the restaurant and the movie."

"You may regret that," he teased.

"Why?"

"Because I'd pick a topless joint and a triple-X-rated movie."

Her mouth opened then closed. He had to be joking. Well, she thought two could play that game. "I know a private club off the interstate where the men take everything off, so we could have dinner and see a show in the same venue."

His laughter, low and husky, floated into her ear. "I don't think so, baby."

"And why not, baby?" she asked in her best West Virginia drawl.

"You really don't expect me to answer that."

"Yeah, I do."

Xavier chuckled. "Maybe some other time. Back to where we can eat. I know it's rather touristy, and a lot of kids hang out there on the weekends, but I like Bubba Gump."

Selena also liked the restaurant chain; the food and service were good and it was within walking distance from her apartment. "Bubba it is. As for movies, we can go to the Terrace out on Maybank Highway. They show movies on either four or five screens. There has to be one or two we can agree on."

"What time should I pick you up?" Xavier asked.

"Eight."

"I'll see you tomorrow at eight. Selena?"

"Yes, Xavier?"

"I've missed you."

"I . . ." Her words trailed off when she heard the distinctive tone indicating he'd hung up on her.

Depressing the button, she ended the connection and returned the receiver to its cradle. Xavier missed her, and Selena did not want to acknowledge that despite her very busy schedule she also missed him.

CHAPTER 11

"Do you have me on speaker?"

"Yes, I do."

"You know I hate it when you do that, Xavier."

"Sorry, Denise, but I can't talk to you and get dressed at the same time." When the phone rang Xavier was tempted not to pick it up until his sister's name appeared on the caller ID display.

"Oh! It's Saturday night and brother love probably has a date."

Sitting on the bench at the foot of his bed, he picked up a pair of socks. "That, Ms. Denise Amaris Eaton, is none of your concern." He wasn't going to confirm his sister's suspicions only because his relationship with Selena was much too new *and* fragile to discuss with anyone. Yes, they'd slept together but that did not translate into commitment. Some women he'd dated casually, never slept with, and yet they were committed to seeing each other exclusively. There were one or two he'd slept with and wasn't bothered if he wasn't the only man she'd shared her body with. Selena Yates was different. He wanted to be the only man she slept with.

The memory of their shower coupling had lingered all week, and it took Herculean strength not to call and ask to see her again. If Selena hadn't told him about her frightening experience with Derrick Perry he would have called. When she'd requested her ex-lover give her some space his reaction was to disappear and then return as a crazed possessive monster. Xavier knew as much as he was beginning to like Selena he would never consciously hurt her — physically or emotionally. And if she decided she didn't want to see him again he would then walk away and relegate her to the other women in his past. And if it were to happen he hoped it would be before he found himself in too deep.

"Don't you mean *biz-ness?*"

Xavier laughed. "If I wanted to say 'biz-ness,' " he drawled, playing along with Denise, "I would've said 'biz-ness.' "

He and Denise had always corrupted the word because a friend of their mother's, who happened to have been a teacher, said 'biz-ness' instead of business. The first time they'd heard her say it they laughed until they'd lost their breath. Hours later Paulette asked what they'd been laughing about and when Denise told her, there was hell to pay for being disrespectful to an adult. Their mother, who'd promised to take them to Disney World for the Christmas recess canceled the trip. It was the first *and* the very last time they'd laughed at anyone. And that included their friends.

"I'm glad to hear that you're dating again," Denise continued in a tone indicating butter wouldn't melt in her mouth. "Where's Garrett?"

"He's in New York on business."

"Something told me he wasn't there with you otherwise we wouldn't be having this conversation." Xavier reached for a pair of khakis. He'd thought about wearing jeans, but then changed his mind. Years of wearing a uniform had spoiled him. It wasn't easy dressing down.

"Why would you say that, Xavier?"

He put one leg into the sharply creased slacks, then the other. "Because you probably would be occupied doing *something* else instead of calling and harassing me."

"Xavier!"

"What, Denise?" he mimicked in falsetto.

"For your information Rhett and I don't spend all our time in bed."

Xavier smiled. "Gotcha! Get your mind out of the gutter, because I wasn't talking about sex."

There came a pregnant pause. "Why am I having this conversation with my brother?"

"Remember, you were the one who mentioned bed, not me."

Picking up a cellophane package, he tore it open and removed a light blue, button-down oxford shirt he'd picked up from the cleaners. When he'd picked up his shirts he'd discovered they weren't on hangers as he'd instructed, but folded and packaged in cellophane. When he told the clerk, she'd offered to have them pressed again and hung on hangers. Instead of going off on the woman he'd asked her to input *Hangers only* into their computerized system under his name.

"You're right. That's not why I called you," Denise continued.

"Why did you call me, baby sis?"

"The desserts Sweet Persuasions shipped to Chandra and Preston were incredible. Chandra couldn't stop talking about them and suggested I use them to make my wedding cake."

Xavier stopped buttoning his shirt. "You

want to order a cake and have it shipped from South Carolina to Pennsylvania?"

Denise sucking her teeth sounded abnormally loud through the speaker. "Couples order wedding cakes from all over the country. So why do you sound so shocked?"

"I don't know," he said, as he finished buttoning his shirt. "I just assumed it would be a crumbled mess by the time you'd get it."

"I'm serious about Sweet Persuasions making my cake. I'm going to call Ms. Yates and set up a time where Rhett and I can come down and sample various fillings. I need to know from you which hotel we should —"

"I know you're not talking about staying in a hotel when I have a house with three extra bedrooms."

"The last time I asked you about your house you told me it was still unfurnished. I'm not one for sleeping on an inflatable mattress in a sleeping bag. Been there, done that."

Xavier laughed. "I've ordered furniture."

"When?"

"This morning."

He'd called the furniture company, placed his order with a salesman, and after his credit card information was checked and approved he was given a delivery date of the following week. He'd arranged for a Thursday afternoon delivery because he only taught one class on Thursdays. Becoming a permanent teacher definitely had its advantages.

"How many months do you have to wait before it's delivered?"

"I should have everything before next weekend. Now, when are you and Rhett coming down?"

"I'll let you know once I talk to Ms. Yates."

"How long do you plan to stay?"

"Probably just for the weekend. We'll drive down Friday and leave Sunday night."

"Why don't you come down for the Columbus Day weekend? That will give us an extra day to be together where I can take you around and show you a little low country hospitality."

Xavier knew the childcare center where Denise was the executive director would close on that day and classes at Christopher Munroe were also cancelled in observance of the holiday. What he didn't tell Denise was that Sweet Persuasions also closed on Mondays.

"That's a wonderful idea. After I talk to Rhett and Miss Yates I'll either call or email you with our plans."

"You can text me."

"Hot damn! Brother love has learned to text."

"Good night, Denise."

"But —"

"I'm hanging up on you. Good night, baby sis."

Pressing a button he ended the call. His sister had teased him relentlessly about his reluctance to text, blog, tweet or Skype. He still hadn't accessed MySpace, or set up a Facebook profile, blog or Twitter account, but occasionally received and sent a text message.

Xavier always enjoyed talking to Denise, but she'd picked the wrong time to call. If he didn't rush he wouldn't get to Selena until well past eight. One thing a life in the military had taught him was to be punctual.

A pair of low-heeled black boots and a navy-blue jacket completed his preppy look. The only thing missing was the requisite striped tie. Dimming the lamp, he walked out of the bedroom. Minutes later he sat behind the wheel of his sports car. It was exactly eight o'clock when the engine roared to life. Traffic permitting, vehicular and pedestrian, he hoped to make it to Selena's apartment within fifteen minutes.

Selena adjusted the hem of her jeans until

they concealed the top of the black leather bootie. She'd fallen in love with the shoes when she first saw them in the window of the shoe store along King Street. The multi-strap, peep-toe boot had a half-inch platform, four-and-a-half-inch heel and back zipper. She peered down at her feet and smiled. The shoes and vermilion color on her toes made her feel unabashedly sexy.

The sound of the building's intercom echoed through the apartment, startling Selena. It was on a rare occasion — a very, very rare occasion that someone rang the bell. The first time it had been college students who'd had too much to drink and were ringing bells up and down the block. The glowing numbers on the clock on the bedside table read 8:00. Xavier said he would pick her up at eight, but he knew to meet in the back and not the front of the building.

She walked out the bedroom to the front door. Punching the button, she said, "Yes." Static and street noises came through the speaker. "Who is it?" she asked.

"Selena Yates?"

"Who is this?"

"Selena Yates?" he repeated.

She released the button. She didn't recognize the masculine voice, and she had no intention of confirming or denying she was Selena Yates. The intercom buzzed again, and Selena ignored it. It buzzed once more and then stopped.

Whoever rang the bell knew her name *and* had to know she occupied one of the two apartments above the patisserie and adjoining gift shop. Although her personal mail bore the address of the second-floor apartment, all packages too large to fit into the vestibule mailbox were delivered to Sweet Persuasions. Maybe the man was a letter carrier or a courier from the shipping company she used for her business.

Then came another ring. This time it was her cell phone. Picking it up off the side table, she answered it. "Hello."

"Hi beautiful. I'm calling to let you know I'm going to be late."

"Where are you, Xavier?"

"I just left my place. I should be there in about ten minutes."

"You'd have to speed to get here in ten minutes. Take your time. I'm not going anywhere."

"I don't want you waiting outside for me. I'll ring your bell and you can buzz me in."

Selena wanted to tell him a man had already rung her bell, asking for her, but didn't want to start in with Xavier about upgrading security for her shop. She hadn't wanted to remind him that she lived on one of the safest streets in the city. Upscale shops and historic inns lined both sides of King Street and there was always a police presence 24/7.

"Okay. See you soon."

"Ditto," Xavier drawled.

The intercom rang for the second time that night, and when Selena answered it she recognized the voice as Xavier's. She opened the door, watching as he climbed the staircase. The adage that absence makes the heart grow fonder was in full effect when she stared at his close-cropped hair and broad shoulders. He raised his head, his eyes meeting hers. There was a message in his deep, penetrating eyes, one she couldn't read or interpret when his expression became a mask of stone. Was he, she mused, as glad to see her as she was him?

Seeing Xavier again made her aware that what she felt for him far exceeded the sex they'd shared. Sex was something she could have with any man. Slaking of sexual frustration could be accomplished with a stranger — someone there for the act — wanting and expecting nothing once it was over. Although she'd told Xavier that she wouldn't be bothered by a one-night stand, she realized she'd lied. She liked and needed him for more than one night and for more than sex.

Grasping his hand, she pulled him inside and closed the door before Monica opened hers. Her neighbor, who had another week off from work, had joined her in the back of the shop Monday afternoon demanding to know who she was dating and if they would see each other again. Selena had given Monica a cursory overview of Xavier's connection to the owners of Ma Bell's and how she'd stepped in as Xavier's date for the restaurant's date night. She didn't tell her that she'd spent the night with Xavier or they'd made love not once, but twice. But she did admit that she liked Xavier — a lot — and she intended to see him again.

"Why on earth are you manhandling me?"

Selena glanced away. "I didn't want my neighbor to see us."

Xavier's eyebrows lifted. "Are you ashamed of being seen with me?"

"Of course not!"

"Then why are you hiding me?"

Her eyelids fluttered wildly. "I am not hiding you, Xavier."

He took a step. "Are you fluttering your lashes hoping I'll succumb —"

"Succumb to what?" Selena interrupted.

Resting his hands at Selena's waist over a white wrap blouse, he stared at her lightly madeup face and the profusion of curls falling around her delicate jaw. "Your attempt to seduce me."

"But . . . but I'm not trying to —"

"You don't have to try, baby," Xavier crooned in her ear. "Isn't the fact that you breathe enough?"

Selena's knees buckled slightly with his passionate revelation. She shook her head, not wanting to believe he'd echoed her feelings. The invisible bond pulling them together wasn't lust or infatuation but something that went beyond a mere liking. For Selena, she realized she was falling in love with a man for the first time in her life.

"Xavier, I thought we were going to take this one day at a time."

He smiled, drawing her intent gaze to the attractive slashes in his jaw. "We have. Yesterday was the day before and this is today. I realized I was attracted to you the moment I walked into your shop and you greeted me with that come-hither voice. And I couldn't believe my luck when Bobby thought I was your so-called mystery boyfriend. The pretense that we were a couple lasted all of three seconds when I drove up and saw you wearing that next-to-nothing skirt and those sexy stilettos. I was giving myself all kinds of kudos because as a leg man you'd made my night."

Her eyes grew wide. "You were thinking all of that?"

Xavier angled his head. "Now, you really don't want to know what I was thinking that night? When you asked me up for coffee it took every ounce of willpower to refuse. You weren't the only one who'd been celibate for a while. There wasn't much I could do with a busted-up leg."

"But . . . but how did you . . . umm . . . get relief?"

Xavier made a fist, moving it back and forth in a shaking motion. "Mother fist and her five daughters."

Selena, when she realized what he'd meant, threw back her head and laughed until her eyes filled with tears. "You're impossible. What am I going to do with you?"

His gaze came to rest on Selena's questioning eyes. "You're going to keep me like I intend to keep you. Let me know now what you want to do. Either we play for keeps, or we can end it right now."

Selena couldn't think straight, not with the sound of her heart pounding in her ears.

"Why are you putting the onus on me?" The query sounded defensive, and at that point she didn't much care.

"I know how I feel about you," Xavier countered, "so the onus has to be on you."

"Doesn't it bother you that we've just met?"

"No more than it bothers me that we slept together four days after our initial meeting. It's not about how much or how little time, but right now, Selena. When I lay in the sand staring up at a man pointing an assault rifle at my head, not once did I think about how much time I had before a bullet stopped my breathing. All I thought of was how am I going to shoot this sonofabitch before he shoots me? That's when I let my eyes roll up in my head, then went completely still. He had to lower his rifle to bend down to see if I was dead and in that split second I pulled out the handgun strapped to my thigh and shot him. I'll never forget the look of shock on his face before he collapsed. I later learned that he was only sixteen. I kept thinking that at sixteen he should've been learning to drive, flirting with girls or maybe having his first sexual encounter. But he wasn't going to be because he'd been forced into adulthood before his time. So, please don't talk to me about time."

Selena bit down on her lip to still its trembling. Xavier had spoken to her if she were a child. "There's no need to chastise me."

"You're wrong, Selena. It is children who are usually chastised. And you're hardly a child." He angled his head, brushing his mouth over hers. "You are a gift, someone who has become special to me."

Anchoring her arms under his shoulders, Selena held on to Xavier as if he'd become her lifeline. She felt the strong steady beating of his heart against her breasts. It was the second time he'd talked about what he'd had experienced as a soldier and it amazed her that he had lain beside her all night without waking up yelling and crying about what he'd seen or done like so many men and women returning from a war zone.

He was right when he'd talked about time. In that split second he could've been killed and she would never know the joy of being in his arms or the passion she'd rediscovered in his embrace.

"Count me in," she whispered.

Pulling back, Xavier stared down at her staring up at him. "For how long?"

"For the duration."

He winked at her. "Always remember that

I'm your man and you're my woman."

She flashed a sexy moue. "What will you do if I have a slight memory lapse?"

"It's not going to happen, because I'm going to remind you every day and every night just how much I've come to love you."

Selena felt her knees buckle, her fingernails biting into solid muscle under the pale blue cotton shirt to help maintain her balance. How could he talk about loving her when . . . Her thoughts stopped as if she'd turned off a faucet, stemming the flow. It was to be another time and she'd come to realize that within the scheme of the universe, she and Xavier were to time like the blink of an eye. They were here, then they were gone.

Did she love Xavier? Yes.

Was she in love with him? She didn't know.

But what she did know was that he'd become so inexorably entwined in her life and she in his that she wanted what they had to continue. Perhaps she'd had to go through what she had with Derrick to appreciate someone like Xavier. He gave her space, space she needed to run her business without the angst she'd had when attempting to memorize countless pages of script. When she and Derrick had gone out together it was always where and what he wanted. He invariably would choose a sushi restaurant with the knowledge she was allergic to raw fish, leaving her to sit and watch him eat while she drank hot sake. There were nights when she'd drunk to forget who he was and could never be.

"I'm going to hold you to that promise," she whispered.

Xavier kissed her again, this time at the corner of her mouth. "Let's go before we won't be able to get a table."

"Do I need a jacket?"

He shook his head. "No, It's still rather warm. But if you get chilled then I'll give you my jacket."

They left, using the back staircase. It was a warm fall night and the streets were filled with throngs taking advantage of the sixty-plus temperatures and the fact that it was a Saturday night. Xavier cradled Selena's hand in the bend of his elbow as they walked to the restaurant that was established after it was introduced in *Forrest Gump.* There was a line outside the restaurant, with an average wait of twenty minutes.

Selena relaxed against Xavier's chest when his arms went around her waist. She hadn't missed the number of women looking at him even when they were with men who appeared to be their dates. She'd engaged in a stare down with one who finally dropped her gaze.

"What was that all about?" Xavier whispered in her ear.

"Nothing."

"It can't be nothing if you're stiff as a board."

Resting the back of her head on his shoulder, she tilted her chin slightly, meeting half-hooded eyes. "I was just wondering how long that heifer was going to keep disrespecting me when she couldn't stop staring at you."

"Sweetheart, she wasn't staring at me."

"Who was she staring at?"

"You."

"No!"

Xavier laughed softly. "Yes. I saw her looking at your shoes, then she decided to check out who's wearing the shoes. Apparently she liked what she saw. I ain't mad at her because we both happen to have exquisite taste."

"But she's here with a man."

Xavier's hands moved up to her arms and he turned Selena around to face him. Having been an actress, he would've thought her more worldly. "And you're here with *your* man, so forget about her."

Selena leaned closer. "If I were your woman, and you were my man, you'd have no other woman, you'd be weak as a lamb," she sang softly, watching Xavier's expression change from amusement to shock.

"Damn, baby. You'd give Gladys Knight a run for her money singing like that."

"Will you be my Pip?"

"I'll be your Pip and if I didn't have a gimpy leg I could also be your backup dancer."

It wasn't until she'd looked closely that Selena had been able to detect the scars under the hair on Xavier's right leg. "You'll do okay as long as you don't crunk."

"Me, crunk? I wouldn't crunk if I had two good legs. I'd be afraid of throwing out my back. I think they're ready for us," Xavier said when he heard a hostess call his name.

They were shown into the restaurant and seated at a table. They were surrounded by tables with raucous students, young children shaking light-up glasses filled with frozen lemon drinks in various colors and a middle-aged couple who appeared unable to keep their hands off each other.

Selena shared a smile with Xavier. "The joint is jumping."

He nodded. "I love the energy."

She agreed. The restaurant was a favorite

with locals and tourists alike. The first time she'd come to Bubba Gump she'd ordered the shrimp po'boy and it had become an instant favorite. The eating establishment was where she'd eaten shrimp and grits for the first time. It, too, became a personal favorite. Occasionally she and Monica, when Trisha would have a sleepover or stay over with her grandparents, would come to the restaurant for a girls' night out. They'd ordered an assortment of appetizers to accompany the potent cocktails they'd drunk like lemonade, then walked home giggling uncontrollably.

Xavier perused the menu. "How hungry are you?"

Selena gave him a sidelong glance. "Hungry enough to order an appetizer and entrée."

"What about dessert?"

"I don't want to see or smell dessert once I leave Sweet Persuasions."

"Speaking of Sweet Persuasions, my sister would like you to make her wedding cake. You have on your website that you do make wedding cakes," Xavier continued when Selena gave him a blank stare.

"Yes, I do." She wondered if Xavier had suggested to his sister that she have a Sweet Persuasions wedding cake in order to steer business her way. “When is her wedding?”

“New Year’s Eve.”

Selena groaned inwardly. Thanksgiving and New Year’s were the two holidays she’d made certain to spend with her family. “Where’s the wedding?”

“Philadelphia. Is that going to pose a problem for you? If it is, then I have to tell Denise to find another pastry chef.”

“No.” And it wouldn’t. She could deliver the cake early that morning or afternoon and still have time to catch a flight to Pikeville, Kentucky where someone would pick her up for the drive to Matewan. “Does she know what type of filling she wants?”

Xavier held up his hands. “I don’t know. She called just before I left to pick you up to say she and her fiancé plan to come down to sample fillings. I suggested they come and stay for Columbus Day weekend. By the way, I’ve ordered the furniture and it will be delivered next Thursday.”

“Do you have an idea how you want to arrange the furniture?”

He stared, complete surprise on his face. Xavier hadn’t thought of it. “No.”

Selena patted his shoulder. “Call me at the shop when the truck arrives and I’ll come over and help out.”

“Who’s going to watch your place?”

"My neighbor is off next week. I'll ask her to man the front for me. If not, then I'll put the Be Back Soon sign on the door."

Cradling her head, Xavier dropped a kiss on her fragrant curls. "I appreciate you offering to help me out, I don't want you to lose money —"

She placed her fingertips over his mouth, stopping his words. "Please let me worry about my bottom line. There are times when I'm forced to close the shop to deliver a special order. If someone wants something, they'll either email or call and leave a message. Remember, I'm selling chocolate, not staples like eggs, bread and milk."

Placing his hand over Selena's, Xavier eased it down. "Don't sleep on chocolate, sweetheart. It served a dual purpose for the Aztecs — food and currency."

"Chocolate has been very good for me, so I'm not discounting its value. In fact, it lives up to the species genus *Theobroma,* which means 'food of the gods.' "

Xavier buried his face in her curls. "One of these days I want you to show me how you make your beautiful edible art."

She closed her eyes, feeling the heat of her lover's breath on her scalp, unable to believe the innocent gesture had aroused her. Her heart rate quickened. "I do most of my baking on Mondays, so whenever we have a three-day holiday weekend you can join me in the kitchen."

"That sounds like a plan." It was the same thing Selena had said to him before she'd agreed to spend the night at his house.

Chapter 12

Monica Mills spread a generous portion of preserves on a slice of whole wheat toast. Taking a bite, she closed her eyes, savoring the piquant flavor of peaches exploding on her tongue and palate.

"Now I know where you got your cooking skills," she said to Selena after swallowing the bread and taking a sip of coffee. "Your grandma's preserves are better than what is on store shelves."

Selena carefully ladled over-easy eggs off the griddle and onto the plate with a sausage link, two strips of crisp bacon and a thinly sliced cured country ham. Whenever she called Monica to ask whether she wanted to share breakfast, her neighbor's response was yes — but only if she prepared the triple pork feast.

Balancing the plate in one hand and a mug of hot tea in the other, she sat down at the table. "I know, and I've told her that.

I've tried talking her into selling them, but she won't budge. My grandmother is sweet as pie and stubborn as a mule."

Monica, her twists held off her round face with a narrow band, shook her head. "She could amass a small fortune if she decided to sell them. So if she does decide to go retail or mail order I could have her talk to one of the lawyers at the firm."

Selena swallowed a mouthful of eggs. "Grandma Lily doesn't trust lawyers. She calls them liars. But, I'm hoping she'll change her mind. That's why I offer samples with new orders or to a new customer, because it translates into free advertising. I'm logging the number of requests for the preserves, and once I reach the projected number of seventy-five I'm going to try and convince Grandma to make enough for Sweet Persuasions — even to sell limited quantities."

"She stands to make a lot of money."

"At seventy-six my grandmother isn't as interested in money as she is making certain her soul is right when the Lord calls her home."

Monica raised her hand in supplication. "Amen. What if she changes her mind and . . . ?"

"What are you trying to say, Monica?"

"What if your grandmother passes? Will you be able to carry on?"

Selena knew if her grandmother did decide to sell her preserves her lifestyle would not change. Lily Yates would continue to live in the garage that had been converted into an apartment for her after her husband of forty-three years passed away, knitting, crocheting, piecing quilts and canning. Lily Yates was an uncomplicated woman living a comfortable, but simple lifestyle.

"No. I never learned canning. Between my mother and grandmother they can fruits and veggies that last from early winter to late spring. The cranberry, onion, kraut and pepper relish is to die for. I'll make certain to bring back a few jars of pickles and relishes the next time I go home."

Monica stared at Selena. Her neighbor had changed. It wasn't her appearance as much as it was her demeanor. She appeared more relaxed, laidback, and Monica wondered if Xavier Eaton was responsible for the subtle transformation.

"You talk about home, Selena, even though you haven't lived there in years, do you still think of West Virginia as your home?"

Selena affected a sad smile. There had been a time when she lived in California, but West Virginia was still home. "It doesn't matter where I list my legal address, Matewan will always be home because my family is there."

Monica waved her fork. "Hypothetically speaking, of course, but if you were to marry Xavier —"

"There is no hypothetical, Miss M. Xavier Eaton and I are dating, not planning a wedding."

Leaning back in her chair, Monica angled her head. "My, my, my," she drawled. "There's no need to get defensive."

"I'm not defensive. I just don't want you to misconstrue things."

Picking up her cup, she stared at Selena over the rim. It wasn't often that they disagreed, and if they did, then it was never about a man. "The only thing I'm going to say and then this discussion is moot — when you do get married I expect to be a bridesmaid."

Selena rolled up a paper napkin, throwing it at Monica. "You'll get married before I do."

Monica rolled her eyes while sucking her teeth. "I don't think so."

"I . . ." The building intercom rang, and the two women looked at each other.

Selena pushed back her chair. It was

eleven o'clock and she didn't expect Xavier to pick her up until two. Before leaving Bubba Gump, Xavier had used his cell phone to check out showtimes, but then realized they wouldn't make the last one on time. He settled the bill and instead of walking back to pick up his car, they'd joined other people strolling the streets and taking in the sights. It was close to midnight by the time they'd returned to her apartment; he escorted her up the staircase, kissed her passionately, then waited until she had closed and locked the door. Peering out the bedroom window, she'd watched as he got into his car and drove away.

She'd discovered walking hand-in-hand down darkened streets, occasionally stopping to peer into windows of shops and talking made her feel as close to Xavier as their lovemaking. She'd heard the excitement in his voice when he talked about teaching. When she'd mentioned that the firing on Fort Sumter by Confederate forces signaled the beginning of the Civil War, it was abolitionist insurgent John Brown's raid on Harpers Ferry in West Virginia that had lit the fuse.

Selena had been astounded when he'd related facts and details of the failed raid, and he reminded her that Robert E. Lee, who had been the arsenal's commander, would become the military leader for the Southern Army two years later. Lee had repelled the insurrection with eighty-eight U.S. Marines, along with members of the Virginia and Maryland militia. Brown's military strength had consisted of sixteen white men, three free blacks, one freed slave and one fugitive slave. She would've been content to walk and talk until the sun came up, but knowing she had to get up early to clean her apartment, put up wash and attend early Sunday-morning service put a halt to their leisurely stroll.

Pressing the button on the panel, she answered the intercom. "Yes." The response was heavy breathing. Selena felt her temper rise. "Idiot!" she screamed into the speaker, then released the button. She would've called whoever rung her bell something more colorful if she'd been alone.

"Who are you calling an idiot?" Monica asked when she rejoined her at the table.

"Someone has been ringing my bell, and when I ask who they are I get nothing."

"I stopped answering my bell, unless I'm expecting someone. Maybe it's because we're on a main drag that people go by and ring all the bells along the street. It's no different from kids getting into an elevator and punching buttons for every floor."

Selena decided she would take Monica's advice and not respond to the intercom. Fortunately for her, she spent a lot of time in the patisserie, even on days when it was closed to the public.

"I can ignore it as long as someone doesn't ring it in the middle of the night."

Monica snorted. "That's when I grab my baseball bat, go out back and introduce whoever is ringing the bell to Louis. And, after I beat the living crap out of him or her, I'll drag them to the corner and leave them for the street sweeper." She'd named her bat Louis because it was a Louisville Slugger. "Don't look at me like that, Selena. I learned to even the odds because I was an only child shorter and smaller than my peers. Thank goodness I've never had to use Louis, but a sister has to think like a scout and Be Prepared. Talking about being prepared, I better leave now and pick up Trisha before I run into traffic." She stood and began clearing the table. "I can't win for losing. I take two weeks off to spend time with my child not realizing she has committed to several sleepover birthday parties."

Selena stared at her petite neighbor as she cleared the table, rinsing and stacking dishes in the dishwasher. Whenever she cooked Monica did the dishes and when Monica cooked she returned the favor. "Do you have anything planned for Thursday?"

Monica halted rising her coffee cup. "No. Why?"

"I'm going to need you to cover me for a few hours, while I make a run."

"No problem. I love working in the shop."

"Thanks, Miss M."

"Girl, please. There's no need to thank me. Not with all you do for my child."

Leaning against the countertop, she watched as Monica made quick work of cleaning the kitchen. Once her neighbor left, she went into the room with a stackable washer and dryer. Opening the dryer, she picked up a wicker basket, filling it with the still-warm garments. After folding laundry she would begin sketching the clown for Carrie Pernell's birthday party.

Selena lay, eyes closed, on a recliner under the tent erected in the rear of the property belonging to Douglas and Leandra Mayer. She'd wanted to get up and go into the house, but somehow she couldn't force her body to follow the dictates of her brain. The loud greetings, deep laughter and backslapping repeated each time someone arrived wearing The Citadel sweatshirt had stopped. The tittering laughter of young children as they chased one another around the backyard, while their parents had called out to them to be careful of knocking over the tables groaning with food or the grills, was missing. All that remained were those who were not too full or hadn't imbibed too much who were talking quietly to the person closest to them with the lingering aroma of grilled food in the humid air.

It wasn't that she'd eaten too much, but the single cup of a liquid stealth, masquerading as rum punch, that had literally put Selena on her back. Although she'd never been much of a drinker, never was it more evident than now. She and Xavier had come to Sandhurst earlier that afternoon to find workmen from a party tent company putting up the tent because meteorologists had forecasted off and on periods of rain throughout the afternoon and early evening.

Bobby Bell had assumed the responsibility, along with his host, to man the grills. Bobby, like all of his former college classmates, wore a sweatshirt commemorating The Citadel. All totaled, Selena had counted eight sweatshirts, including the one Xavier sported proudly, and two others worn by toddlers announcing they were future cadets of the prestigious military college.

The cookout menu included the ubiquitous ribs, steaks, chicken, hamburgers and franks, along with side dishes of potato salad, macaroni and cheese, slaw, and a large bowl of mixed green salad. A portable bar had been set up under the tent with a sign that read Adults Only, while the young children were offered a cooler chest filled with prepackaged fruit juices.

"Are you all right, baby?"

Selena opened one eye, then the other, peering at Xavier, who lay on his side staring at her. "I'll let you know tomorrow."

"What's the matter?"

She smiled. "The punch knocked me out. I'm down for the count."

Resting his head on a folded arm, Xavier's gaze moved lovingly over Selena's composed features. The humidity had curled the hair that had escaped the ponytail, wisps sticking to her moist face. He'd closely watched the reaction of his former college classmates when he'd introduced them to her. A few had held on to her hand a little longer than was socially correct, but all had given her their best toothpaste smiles.

"But, you only had one cup."

"What I shouldn't have had was that one cup. You should know by now that I'm not much of a drinker."

Xavier gave her a tender smile. "That's all right. I still love you."

Selena closed her eyes against his intense stare. It was much too easy for her to get caught up in the illusion that Xavier was in love with her. And what she didn't want to do was confuse an intense liking with love. Too often people glibly said "I love this" or "I love that" when they actually meant they were fond, partial or had taken a fancy to someone. She'd equated love to feeling deep affection, or falling in love.

She opened her eyes, her gaze as soft as a caress. "Love you back," she whispered.

"Do you?"

The two words were spoken so softly Selena thought she'd imagined them. "Do I what?"

"Do you love me?"

Selena's heart jolted. *Why here? Why now?* she mused. Why had Xavier picked a public place, a place where people knew him, to ask her such a leading and personal question? "Do you expect me to answer that?"

"Yes, I do."

"Are you always this direct?" she accused.

Xavier's expressive eyebrows lifted a fraction. "That's the only way I know how to be. Now, please answer the question. Do you love me, Selena?" He'd enunciated each word.

The initial attraction she'd felt for Xavier deepened and intensified every time she saw him. Whenever he called, the sound of his sonorous voice and passionate greeting lingered with her for hours. Unknowingly he had unlocked her heart making it possible for her to learn to trust again, and more importantly fall in love. The time in which they'd known each other no longer mattered. And whenever she recalled their passionate coupling her body reacted violently — aching for his touch.

Selena kept telling herself it was because he was eye candy, the subtle arrogance that had come from his military training that drew her to him. And as much as she'd tried coming up with excuses as to why she would sleep with a stranger, none offered the ease she sought. She opened her mouth, but nothing came out.

Xavier sat up, swinging his legs over the side of the recliner. "Breathe, Selena."

It wasn't until Xavier told her to breathe that she realized she'd been holding her breath. "Yes," she gasped. "Yes, I love you."

Pushing to his feet, Xavier reached down and gently pulled her to stand. Wrapping his arms around her body, he pressed her to his length. He pressed a kiss to her moist forehead. Holding Selena, feeling the runaway beating of her heart against his chest and inhaling the sensual fragrance of her perfume clinging to her velvety skin filled him with a peace he hadn't thought possible.

He, who'd run from love like a coward retreating in battle, had rushed straight into the arms of a woman who was as different from the others in his past as night was from day. With other women it had been what he wanted: he didn't want to get too serious, didn't want to marry, didn't want to become a father and couldn't commit because he didn't know where he would be stationed or reassigned, or when he would be deployed. He had more excuses for not loving a woman as there were stars in the sky or grains of sand on the beach.

Xavier had asked himself over and over what made him walk into Sweet Persuasions that momentous morning and the answer was the same: fate, destiny or providence. They were all one in the same.

His hand moved up and down her back in a soothing motion. "It's going to be good."

Pulling back, Selena searched his face for a hint of guile. His gaze was steady and there was no tension in his jaw. The tense lines in her own face relaxed when she realized she was being offered a second chance, a chance to love and, more important, trust.

She scrunched her nose. "You promise?"

A smile tilted the corners of Xavier's firm mouth. "I promise."

"Yo, X-man. Somebody needs your lady to come inside."

He turned to find Bobby gesturing to him." He smiled at Selena. "That'd be *you,* sweetheart," he teased. He watched Selena as she walked out of the tent to where Bobby stood waiting for her. Xavier reuniting with his former classmates made him feel as if he'd truly come home. To say he'd missed them was an understatement — especially Bobby.

Robert Bell had been granted a medical discharge after he was diagnosed with an irregular heartbeat. The news had devastated Bobby, who'd planned to become a lifer. He'd loaded up his car with the intent of fulfilling a wish to visit all fifty states. Once he made it to California, he parked his car in the airport parking lot and boarded a plane for a flight to Hawaii.

A mechanical problem during the return drive changed Bobby and his life forever. He broke down outside of Vegas, which forced him to spend nearly a week in the city while the mechanic awaited the delivery of the replacement part. Bobby met a woman who'd come to Vegas for her wedding, but her fiancé sent her a voice mail message that he'd changed his mind and couldn't marry her. Bobby found her in a bar, crying and drinking. He'd managed to get her to open up to him and he and the operating room nurse, who had grown up in foster homes, spent the next twelve hours talking. They exchanged phone numbers, promising to keep in touch.

The number of calls between Indianapolis and Charleston increased from once a week to every night within the span of a month. When Bobby got into his car to take another road trip his intent was to propose marriage. After securing a license, they'd exchanged vows at the courthouse. Bobby stayed in Indianapolis long enough for Chandra to resign her position at a municipal hospital; she sold her car, gave up her apartment and moved to Charleston as Mrs. Robert Bell. That was four years ago. The Bells were the proud parents of a three-year-old daughter and two-month-old son.

Selena's hand was lost in Bobby's massive grip when he led her into the kitchen where

Leandra sat at the kitchen table with a young woman with unruly copper curls; her gaze went to the toddler on her lap with the same flyaway hair but in a lighter, brighter shade.

Bobby released Selena's hand. "I'll see you later."

Turning, she watched his broad shoulders as he walked out of the kitchen, then directed her attention to the two women. "Did someone want to see me about something?"

Leandra patted the chair beside her. "Please come and sit down. I know you met Ellie, but I don't know if you know what she does for a living," she said to Selena when she joined them at the table.

Selena smiled at Ellie, noticing for the first time the spray of freckles covering her nose and cheeks. Like the other women in attendance, she was married to one of Xavier's former college classmates. "No, I don't."

Elaine McKinney rocked her son gently, her eyes meeting those of the woman whose life would change appreciably after hearing her proposal. "Lee told me you made the desserts."

Selena nodded. "Yes, I did."

"I'm going to propose something to you and I'm going to need your answer like yesterday."

Now, her curiosity was piqued. "I can't give you an answer until I know what it is you're proposing."

Ellie's clear brown eyes met Leandra's. "I'm a producer for a new show on the Travel Channel that will feature different cities throughout the country. My first choice is Charleston. I've chosen this city not only because I live here, but it is also one of the most popular Southern destinations in the country. When I saw your chocolate desserts the first thing that came to mind is that they're too pretty to eat." She blushed. "But, of course I couldn't resist eating just one, which quickly became two, three and etcetera. I'm saying all this because I'd like to include Sweet Persuasions in the segment."

Selena stared at Ellie, complete surprise freezing her features. She didn't know what to expect, but it was not an opportunity to have her patisserie featured on a popular cable channel. "This is a lot to take in all at once."

Ellie smiled. "I know it sounds a little overwhelming."

"It's more than a little," she countered. Her impulse was to refuse, but Selena had worked too hard, put in too many long hours not to take advantage of an opportunity akin to a blessing.

"The reason I need your answer is because the restaurant we'd filmed had a fire a couple of weeks ago, and the damage was pretty extensive. I've been looking for a worthy replacement but hadn't found one until now. Lee let me use her computer and I searched your website. A Parisian patisserie with bistro tables, delicate pastries and chocolates and the espresso machine is exactly what I'm looking for. Even the blue-and-white decor is Francophile. If you approve, then I'll have a film crew here tomorrow."

Selena was confused. When Ellie had mentioned she needed her answer "like yesterday" she actually meant it. "Why the rush?"

"The segment is scheduled to air in two weeks. That's just enough time for us to film and edit what should go into the piece."

It was the first time in a very long time that Selena found herself in a quandary. Millions of viewers tuned in to the Travel Channel and to have them film Sweet Persuasions was an opportunity that would probably only come once.

"How long will it take to complete the segment?"

"I estimate anywhere between three and

four hours. It could go longer if you have customers."

"Customers will not pose a problem, because I close on Mondays. It's the day when I do most of my baking for the week."

Ellie kissed her fingertips. "*Perfecto!* Then it shouldn't take more than a couple of hours." She extended her right hand. "Do we have a deal?"

Selena looked at Ellie, then Leandra, who gave her wink, then her gaze swung back to the television producer. She shook her hand. "Yes."

Ellie shifted the sleeping child on her lap to a more comfortable position. "I'm going to call the network lawyer and have him download a contract to you. If you have an attorney, then I want you to have them look it over. Once we get your approval we'll include your patisserie in the show. I'm going to warn you in advance that once it airs you're going to have to prepare yourself for a dramatic spike in business."

"I'll be ready," Selena said with more confidence than she actually felt at that moment. If Ellie was right, then it would mean her hiring an assistant and someone to take care of the front. And there was the possibility she would also have to hire a delivery person.

Smiling, Elaine McKinney stood up. "I better put this boy down. My mother-in-law holds him while he's sleeping, but what Master McKinney doesn't understand is that his mama is not his grandma."

It took Leandra a little longer to come to her feet. She wore a colorful kente cloth smock over a pair of black leggings. "Let me show you where you can put him down."

She smiled at Selena. "I bought a queen-size inflatable mattress for the kids to sleep on after I realized how many of us have children. Luckily Bobby and Chandra bought a portable crib for their son, or he would have to share the mattress with the other toddlers."

Selena nodded, smiling. She would thank Lee later, once she got her alone. If she hadn't ordered dessert from Sweet Persuasions, then the producer from the Travel Channel would've never approached her.

Hanging out with Xavier Eaton had its advantages. Advantages that would no doubt prove to be ongoing.

Selena pulled Xavier into her apartment, closing and locking the door behind them. Jumping up into his arms, she looped her legs around his waist, planting noisy kisses all over his face.

"Thank you, thank you, thank you!"

Anchoring his arms around her waist, Xavier gave Selena a puzzled look. "Hold up, baby. I don't mind you kissing me, but I would like to know what you're thanking me you for."

Pressing her mouth to his ear, she told him about Elaine McKinney's offer. "My initial impulse was to say no. But then I thought about it. Not only would it be free advertising, but also a way I can grow my business." She mentioned hiring employees, the words falling over one another as her head worked faster than her mouth. "What do you think, Xavier? Do you think I did the right thing accepting her proposal? If I hadn't met you then I never would've met Ellie."

Xavier rested his forehead on Selena's. "It would've eventually happened. You're an incredible businesswoman. But, if you want to give me kudos, then I graciously accept it. However, I can think of another way you can thank me." His voice had lowered seductively.

Peering at him through her lashes, Selena stared at the shape of Xavier's mouth. "How?"

He angled his head, whispering in her ear

what he wanted from her. "Are you up for it?"

Her smile was dazzling. She tightened her grip on his neck. "I believe I am. Do you know the story of *Hansel and Gretel*?"

"Refresh my memory."

"Put me down and I'll show you."

Chapter 13

Xavier lowered Selena until her feet touched the cool surface of the wood floor. He watched, transfixed as she slipped out of her running shoes. He wasn't certain what she intended to do as she backpedaled, her hands going to the buttons on her blouse. She stopped, slipped out of the blouse, leaving it on the floor. His breathing quickened when he stared at the swell of breasts rising above the lacy cups of a white demi-bra. Even in the diffused light coming from a table lamp he could detect a come-hither look in her eyes.

Xavier moved off the door, following as if pulled along by an invisible wire. Selena undressing slowly and methodically taking off each article of clothing as if she were on a burlesque stage was a definite turn-on. He liked her like this — playful *and* sexy.

His hands went to his belt, undoing the buckle. "Now I remember *Hansel and Gretel,* but isn't this more like the *Pied Piper of Hamelin*?" His belt hit the floor.

Reaching out, her fingertips trailing along the wall to guide her, Selena's gaze fused with Xavier's. "No, darling. The pied piper drove the rats out of town by playing a flute. And you're hardly a rodent."

"If I were an animal, what would I be?" He'd pulled the sweatshirt over his head, it, too, landing on the floor.

Selena unsnapped the waistband to her walking shorts, leaning against the wall to keep her balance when she pushed them down her hips and stepped out of them. "Wolf," she crooned.

"Why a wolf?"

"In Native American animal medicine the wolf represents teacher or pathfinder."

Xavier kicked off his running shoes. "What about a hawk?"

"Mmm-hmm. Hawk. I think it means perspective."

"Nah. I don't like hawk as much as wolf." He closed the distance between them. "How about one more?"

"Instead of a hawk you could be a falcon. A falcon represents success, restraint and accuracy."

Xavier ran the back of his hand over her

delicate jaw. "Which animal are you, Selena?"

Resting her hands over his pectorals, Selena kissed the colored tattoo. "I'm a bluebird — content, happy and filled with an indescribable joy that makes me want to pinch myself to see if I'm dreaming. And if I am, then I never want to wake up."

Looping an arm around her waist, Xavier took possession of her mouth like a man dying of thirst thrusting his face in a cold, running stream. Her lips parted under the sensual onslaught, giving him free rein, his tongue plunging in and out of her mouth and simulating his making love to her.

Lifting her, Selena's bare feet dangling inches above the floor, he walked slowly, backing her into the bedroom. The waning daylight coming through the lacy panels at the windows provided enough light for Xavier to identify the objects in the room. He wanted this coming together to be different than what they'd shared in the shower. That coupling had been spur of the moment, unbridled and totally uninhibited. This time when he made love with Selena he wanted a slow exploration, a dreamy intimacy that would remain when separated. He swept back the quilt and coverlet, placing Selena on the cool, crisp sheets.

Selena felt as if she was on fire. The swath of heat that began in her feet swirled up her body, stopping momentarily at her core before moving upward. Closing her eyes, she let her senses take over. She heard, rather than saw, Xavier unzip his jeans, the rustling of fabric as he pushed them off his hips. He moved slightly, his erection brushing her inner thigh. She listened intently, recognizing the sounds when he opened the condom packet, smiling when he rolled the sheath down his erection.

While she enjoyed making love with Xavier, she wasn't ready to deal with an unplanned pregnancy. It wasn't that she was opposed to marriage and motherhood, but there was no way she would be able to balance marriage, motherhood and run a retail business. Perhaps it was time she see her gynecologist about prescribing an oral contraceptive.

Nude and resplendently aroused, Xavier knelt over Selena. He showered kisses over her eyelids, along the column of her neck and on her shoulders. Reaching under her back, he unhooked her bra, tossing it on the floor beside the bed. "I like it," he crooned, his tongue sweeping over her breast. "I like this one, too," he continued, giving the other equal attention. Anchoring his hands under the narrow waistband of her bikini panties, his fingers traced the outline of her bottom, lingering along the indentation separating the two spheres of firm muscle before removing the triangle of lace and silk. "You are so special, so very special to me," he whispered over and over, placing feathery kisses down the length of her body.

Selena thought she was going to shatter into a million pieces when his hand searched between her thighs. Arching off the mattress, she shivered, shuddering violently as he resumed his manual and oral exploration. Why, she thought, was he torturing her? She gasped when the flame he'd ignited inside her threatened to consume her — whole.

"Please."

Xavier answered her plea, positioning his sex at her wet, pulsing entrance and pushing gently. His own groan echoed her gasps as he felt her body opening, stretching. It appeared to be minutes, but in actuality it was only seconds before he'd buried his sex deep enough to touch her womb. Her body was tight — inside and out.

He began to move, rolling his hips.

He called. She answered.

She beckoned. He came.

Everything faded for Selena — everything

except the man lying between her thighs and transporting her to place where she soared like a falcon, gliding on air currents. Then it happened. Whimpers of ecstasy escaped her when the first orgasm seized her, the pressure building steadily with her lover's powerful thrusting.

Holding her head firmly between his hands, Xavier pulled back and drove his swollen flesh into Serena's wet, pulsing body. Without warning, the dam broke. Burying his face between her scented neck and shoulder, he bellowed his explosive triumph of surrender into the pillow while Selena sobbed out her shivering delight against his shoulder.

They lay motionless and breathing heavily, savoring the aftermath of completion. When she did move it was to trail her fingertips over Xavier's damp back. He'd become her lover *and* her man.

Xavier's breathing finally slowed and he gathered enough strength to reverse their positions. Pulling Selena close, he reached down and drew the sheet up over their bodies. Not only had he fallen in love with her — but he also loved her.

Reuniting with the cadets from his graduating class, and seeing them with their wives, children and girlfriends, was a reminder of if it hadn't been for the corps his life would've had no purpose. Some were still active military, while others had gone on to have successful careers as civilians. Ellie's husband was in the military police before he left the army to join the Charleston Police Department. He, who had always avoided commitment, was now ready to commit. He, who had lived his life serving his country, wanted what Bobby, Doug and the others had. He wanted a family of his own.

Selena woke early Monday morning to find Xavier asleep beside her. Rising on an elbow, she peered at the clock on the bedside table. It was minutes after four. She got out of bed without waking him and walked into the bathroom for her morning ablution.

The light from the lamp on the table outside the bedroom provided enough illumination for her to see that Xavier had shifted position, lying on his back, chest rising and falling in a slow, even rhythm when she returned to the bedroom.

"You smell delicious."

Selena smiled. "I didn't know you were awake."

"I woke up when you got out of bed."

Xavier's voice sounded disembodied in the darkened space.

"I'm sorry," she apologized as she approached the bed.

Xavier sat up, stretching like a large cat. "Don't be. It's time I get up and head home."

"Do you want to stay long enough for me to fix you breakfast?"

Reaching over he turned on the lamp, then swung his legs over the side of the bed. "No, thank you. I'll eat on campus."

Selena tightened the belt to her wrap around her waist. She watched as he searched the bed and floor for his underwear and jeans. The muscles in his back rippled sensuously under his skin when he bent over to put on his pants.

"You'll find the rest of your clothes on the bench next to the table in the hall."

Turning, Xavier's teeth shone whitely when he looked at her. "Gretel was a very naughty girl last night. If I remember correctly, wasn't Hansel her brother?"

Resting her hands at her waist, Selena glared at him. "What are you trying to say? That I stripped for my brother?"

"Let's say the next time we play fairy tales, you pick one with a big-bad wolf."

"But the wolf always eats someone."

Xavier winked at her. "That's why I like being the wolf. Not only do you smell delicious, but you also taste delicious."

Selena's breathing quickened, her cheeks burning in remembrance of the first time Xavier had made love to her. "Go home, Xavier." She wanted him to go before she begged him to make love to her again.

Xavier winked again, knowing he'd embarrassed Selena. There were times when she was so worldly that he'd forgotten how young she was. Then without warning, she appeared the ingenue, demure and blushing.

"I'm going," he said, brushing past her as he left the bedroom. "I'll call you later."

His departing words stayed with her until she unlocked Sweet Persuasions, disarmed the alarm, reset it and walked to the rear of the shop to check the voice mail and email.

As promised, Ellie had sent her the contract, which she promptly downloaded and printed. The producer had also left a voice mail message saying the film crew would arrive at ten, but she'd be there around nine.

Selena added four new mail-order requests to her calendar. Sighing, she stared at the wall calendar. She kept two calendars — one on the computer and the other on the wall, the latter acting as backup if or when she lost internet service. Staring at the notations on the calendar was like someone banging a gong, the sound reverberating and shaking her to the core. Selena realized she'd been in denial and avoiding the inevitable. She had to hire an assistant pastry chef. There was no way she was going to continue at the current pace, trying to balance her business, personal and social life. It hadn't been as apparent before she'd begun seeing Xavier. As it was they only saw each other on the weekend when she would've liked to see him at least one day during the workweek. Reaching for a square of notepaper from a plastic cube, she jotted: "pastry school intern." The note square went up on the bulletin board with others in differing colors.

She went through her Monday-morning ritual of wiping down the bistro tables, chairs, cleaning showcases, the espresso machine, the minuscule bathroom and sweeping and mopping floors. After she'd stored the cleaning supplies in a utility closet she added another colorful square to the bulletin board: "part-time maintenance." Running a small business in Charleston had its advantages because it was a college city and students who needed extra money were usually willing to take on a part-time position.

Selena switched on the audio system, tuning the satellite radio to a station featuring Motown favorites. She'd grown up listening to the music from the '60s, '70s and '80s, music her parents had grown up with. Much to her chagrin, Selena knew the lyrics to Stevie Wonder and Earth, Wind & Fire's greatest hits.

Fortified with a cup of tea with lemon and a slice of chocolate-almond cake with candied orange peel, she slipped the apron over her head, tying it at the waist, covered her hair with a bouffant cap and began the task of tempering couverture chocolate for the rabbit party favors. She projected it would take her all day to make sixty molded rabbits. Then she would concentrate on making the clown centerpiece, an assortment of molded candies with fabulous fillings, exotic treats with varying decorations and finally the cakes and tortes. Working as a chocolatier called for an attention to detail. The finished product had to look as good as it would taste.

The shop phone rang and Selena picked up before the second ring. "Good morning, Ms. M."

"How did you know it was me?"

She smiled. "It's because I'm clairvoyant."

"Caller ID clairvoyant."

"Damn! I'm busted again. What's up, Monica?"

"I just put Trisha on the bus and I want to know if you need help this morning."

Selena opened her mouth to decline her friend's offer, then rethought her decision. "I need a different kind of help."

"Open the door, Selena."

"Come around back." She went to the rear of the shop, disarmed the alarm, then reset it when Monica walked in. "I have a contract I'd like you to look at before I take it to my attorney."

Dressed in a pale-gray sweatsuit and matching running shoes, Monica rested her hands at her narrow hips. "If I've told you once, I've told you ad nauseam to stop giving that man your hard-earned money. I've told the men at the firm that you're my cousin and they believe it because they've heard Trisha talk about Titi Selena. One of the perks is I'm allowed a special hourly rate for one family member."

Selena crossed her arms under her breasts over the bibbed apron. "What is the family rate?"

The paralegal made a circle with her thumb and forefinger. "Zero."

"Zero?"

"What don't you understand, Selena? The *z,* or the *o?*" She held out her hand. "Please give me the contract."

Monica took the stack of paper. "If you don't mind I'm going to fix myself a cup of coffee while I read this." Her eyes narrowed when she read the first line. "What's happening with Sweet Persuasions and the Travel Channel?"

Selena told her friend about her meeting with the television producer, smiling when Monica's expression changed from shock to tearful joy. "Ellie should be here in about twenty minutes and the film crew at ten."

"Here! This morning?"

Selena nodded. "Yes."

"Omigosh! Oh, mercy!" Monica chanted. "You're going to be on television?"

"Not me, Monica. Sweet Persuasions."

"Don't play yourself, Selena. You *are* Sweet Persuasions. You work as hard as a pack mule spending countless hours making the most incredibly decadent confectionery imaginable. I've never seen or heard you go off on some of the most annoying people I've had the misfortune of meeting. We all know how difficult it is to run a successful small business nowadays, but either you're blessed or just plain lucky. You deserve only the best life has to offer. Try to enjoy it, girlfriend."

Extending her arms, Selena hugged Monica. "Thank you for being you."

"And thank you for being my BFF."

A tapping on the front door glass caught their attention. "That's the show's producer," Selena said when she saw Ellie's face pressed against the glass. Disarming the security system, she opened the door, smiling. "Good morning. Please come in." She had tamed her curls with gel, brushing them off her face, put on a tailored, navy pantsuit and white blouse, that replaced the T-shirt and jeans she'd worn to the Mayers' cookout.

Elaine McKinney walked in, her gaze sweeping around the confectionery shop. "Good morning. I'm a little early, but I wanted to get here to look around."

"I'd like you to meet my cousin, Monica Mills. Monica, Elaine McKinney. Monica works for the firm that will review the contract." The two women exchanged the requisite greetings and handshakes.

Ellie rested her tote on the floor. "Do you mind if I look around?"

"Not at all. Would you like some coffee or tea before the others get here?" Selena asked when she saw her glance at the coffee machine.

"I'd love some," Ellie crooned.

Monica winked at Selena. "I'll make it."

Ten minutes later the three women sat at a table sipping hot beverages, while Ellie and Monica nibbled on delicate heart-shaped butter cookies. By the time the film crew arrived, Sweet Persuasions claimed an autumnal ambience with orange votives on each table, a door wreath with leaves in colors of red, bright orange, yellow and brown and the shelves in the showcases were lined with orange-and-black lace doilies. If agreed upon, the segment would air a week before Halloween.

Selena opened storage containers of decorative candies with black and orange jelly beans, candy corn and M&M's, sprinkling them on the doilies before placing parchment lined trays of chocolate-covered candies, fruit, cookies, nuts and individual servings of cheesecake, brownies, tortes and mousse. The only thing missing was candied jelly apples. She'd changed her apron to one with blue-and-white stripes monogrammed with Sweet Persuasions on the bib, and a white toque had replaced the nylon bouffant cap.

The crew arrived, along with a makeup

person and the show's host, a perky young woman with a toothpaste-ad smile who introduced herself as Becca. Ellie gave her the background information on the patisserie that had become a favorite with Charlestonians since its spring opening.

Selena was filmed fastening two halves of the rabbit molds with clips and half filling it with tempered couverture. She was directed to look at the camera when asked to explain *couverture.*

It was as if time had stood still when she looked at the camera and like she was on the set of the daytime soap delivering her lines on cue. She knew her best angles and had mastered voice modulation. Although she'd walked away from an acting career, she was still an actress.

She affected a sensual smile. "The technical name for the type of chocolate used to make chocolate bars and candies, icings and cream filling is couverture. It contains cocoa butter, sugar, vanilla, cocoa solids and lecithin. It is delicious and can be eaten without further processing."

"What about white chocolate?" Becca asked.

"White chocolate isn't really chocolate."

"But why it is called chocolate?"

The cameraman pulled back to get both

of them in the shot. "It's made from cocoa butter, but lacks the components that give cocoa its color and taste and, for this reason, legally must be called white confectionery coating."

The filming continued for another two hours while Selena prepared ganache cream, sweetened with fondant and combined with a generous amount of butter to make cognac balls and kirsch rolls. Becca responded enthusiastically when Selena filled a pastry bag with tempered couverture, piping it to create a chocolate lattice, flower petals and drops and buttons. She demonstrated a basic recipe for drinking chocolate using a vanilla bean, bitter chocolate and sugar, topping it with whipped cream and grated chocolate.

The taping ended and Selena handed out cups of chocolate to the crew before she removed the toque and flopped down to a chair at the bistro table. It had gone longer than she'd expected. Her eyes met Ellie's. "I know not everything is going to air."

"I'll look at it carefully and decide what should stay and what will be edited out." Ellie took a sip of hot chocolate. "If I'm not careful I'm going to turn into a chocoholic."

Selena smiled. "That's why I rarely touch the stuff. Cocoa beans contain caffeine and theobromine, which is a close relative of caffeine and is used in medicine as both a stimulant and diuretic."

Ellie took another swallow. "If I keep drinking this I'll never lose the ten pounds that hang on to my hips like a needy friend." She glanced at her watch. "I have to go, but I'll be in touch with you. Please have your attorney review the contract and let me know if it's a go. Meanwhile, I'll go over the tape."

"What's the projected date for airing?"

Reaching for her tote, Ellie took out her planner. "Thursday, October 22. It will air in the eight o'clock time slot on the east coast."

Selena gave her a warm smile. It would air four days after her twenty-seventh birthday — a birthday she would always remember.

Chapter 14

Late Sunday morning Xavier waited in the doorway, watching his future brother-in-law assist Denise from the car. He hadn't seen his sister since the summer, and he had to admit she looked well. He'd expected them to arrive either late Friday or Saturday morning, but Denise had called to say that Garrett had to take care of a family crisis, and she would explain when she saw him.

When Denise tucked chin-length, blunt-cut hair behind her left ear as she stood looking up at the two-story white house with black shutters, framing tall, narrow windows, late-morning sunlight glinted off the large diamond on her hand. Xavier had attempted to describe a Charleston single house but his description fell far short of the structure with white porches behind a decorative wrought-iron fence.

Pushing his hands into the pockets of his slacks, Xavier rocked back on his heels. "Are you going to stay there all morning gawking?"

Denise smiled at her brother. "I wasn't gawking. I was just looking at your house."

"Look at it later. I have brunch waiting for you and Garrett."

Garrett Fennell took his fiancée's hand, leading her to where her brother stood waiting for them. "Now you're talking." He extended his free hand to Xavier. "Thanks for inviting us."

Xavier shook the proffered hand. "Welcome to Charleston."

His gaze shifted from Garrett to Denise. They made the perfect couple. He'd thought that six years ago, and it was no different now. Garrett was only twenty-eight and a self-made millionaire, and although casually dressed, there was something about the young businessman extraordinaire that radiated power and confidence. The last time Xavier saw him he was clean-shaven. Now he wore a neatly barbered mustache and goatee.

Xavier took a step, picked up Denise and swung her around the way he'd done when they were younger. Whenever he came home on military leave he would swing her around and around until she begged him to stop. And he would stop, let her go and watch as she attempted to regain her balance.

Pressing his mouth to her ear, he whispered, "I hope I didn't hurt the baby."

Denise went completely still, then landed a punch on his shoulder. "Bite your tongue, Xavier Philip Eaton."

Smiling, his eyebrows lifted. "Well, are you in the family way?"

She rolled her eyes at him. "No. And, we've decided to wait. Now that puts the pressure on you to make Mom a grandmother."

Xavier kissed his sister's cheek. "Not even close." He lowered her to stand. "Where are your bags?" He noticed Garrett hadn't opened the trunk of the Mercedes-Benz.

Garrett met Xavier's questioning expression. "I wish Denise and I could stay but we have to get back to D.C. tonight."

Xavier angled his head. He didn't know what was going on, but he intended to find out. "Come inside and we'll talk about it over brunch."

Denise and Garrett shared a look, then followed Xavier inside. He'd issued an order. Raising her hand, she got off a snappy salute.

"I saw that," Xavier said over his shoulder.

"Don't tell me you have eyes in the back of your head?"

"I have superpowers I haven't even begun to use," he teased.

"Oh, my goodness!" Denise gasped. "These sweetgrass baskets are beautiful." She stared at the number of handmade baskets lining a rustic drop leaf table in the entryway, then up at the hanging gaslight fixture, reminiscent of a bygone era.

"You can't live in the low country and not own a sweetgrass basket." Xavier repeated what Selena had told him.

Denise slowed, glancing around the living room. "What decorating firm did you use?"

"I didn't use a firm."

"Who picked out the furniture?"

"A friend." Turning around, Xavier held up his hand. "I'll tell you everything once I take you on a tour of the house." He turned again, heading in the direction of the kitchen.

Garrett sniffed the air. "Something smells good."

"I figured you'd be hungry, so I prepared brunch. You guys can wash up over there." Xavier pointed to a door at the far end of the spacious kitchen.

Over a sumptuous brunch of bacon, breakfast links, country ham, grits, eggs, corned beef, hash, miniature corn muffins, butter and a variety of jellies, preserves and jams served in the kitchen's dining area, Xavier listened, stunned by the news that Trey Chambers, Sr., who'd had a heart attack earlier that summer, had not survived a second one. This news did not shock Xavier as much as the revelation that the real-estate mogul was Garrett Fennell's biological father.

Garrett stared at the residue of coffee in his cup. "There will be no funeral, just a private graveside service tomorrow morning."

Xavier shook his head. "When I read that Capital Management had gone into partnership with Chambers Properties, I thought it was just another successful deal for your company. I had no idea it was family related."

An audible sigh slipped passed Garrett's lips. "My mother kept my paternity a secret for twenty-six years, and probably would've for another two decades if the attorney handling Trey Chambers, Sr.'s legal affairs hadn't requested I be present at the reading of the will."

Xavier touched the corners of his mouth with a damask napkin. Selena had insisted he use cloth napkins rather than paper, which she claimed should only be used during outdoor cookouts or large gatherings.

"How is Trey, Jr.?" he asked, aware that Denise, Garrett and the younger Chambers had been inseparable when they attended Johns Hopkins.

Denise placed her hand on her fiancé's. "He's coping, although he'd asked Rhett to make funeral arrangements."

"Do you want me to come up for —"

"No," Garrett said, protesting and interrupting Xavier. "It's absurd to drive hundreds of miles for a twenty-minute service. We wouldn't have come down if we hadn't committed to the wedding-cake tasting."

Xavier checked his watch. "We have three hours before we have to leave for Sweet Persuasions. Meanwhile, you can relax in one of the guest bedrooms." He knew Denise and Garrett had gotten up early to make the more than five-hundred-mile drive from D.C. to reach Charleston before eleven.

Denise rose to her feet. "Rhett, why don't you go up and relax. I'll be up as soon as I look around." She'd noticed a change in her fiancé when he'd gotten the news that his biological father had died. He hadn't said it, but she knew he regretted not having a relationship with the man who'd seduced his innocent teenage mother, while he was engaged to another woman.

"When you go up the stairs it's the last bedroom on the right," Xavier said. Waiting until Garrett walked out of the kitchen, he approached his sister, hugging her. "How is *he* doing?"

Leaning back in her brother's embrace, Denise stared up at him. "Rhett is Rhett. There are times when he shuts me out, and I wait for him to open up."

"Does he?"

Denise nodded. "Most times he does. It's different this time because it's not business but personal. It's very different for him than it was for us because we grew up with our father. It has to be devastating for Rhett to spend the more than twenty-five years wondering who his father is, and when he does find out he's unable to have any type of relationship with him because three months later he's dead."

"He's lucky he has you."

"We're both lucky. What about you? How's the leg?"

"My leg is good. It tells me when it's going to rain or when I've overdone it, but all in all it serves me well."

Denise pulled out of his loose embrace. "I know you're probably going to tell me to mind my business and that I'm being like

Paulette Eaton, but are you seeing anyone?"

Instead of lying to his sister, Xavier had chosen to evade her questions or circumvent the truth by asking her a similar question. This time he didn't want to do either, because it would be like denying what lay in his heart.

"Yes, I'm seeing someone."

"Is she good to you?"

"She's good *for* me, Denise."

"Good for you, brother love."

"Come, let me show you the house, then I want you to rest before we leave."

Denise looped her arm through Xavier's. "You have to give me the name of your decorator. I keep telling Rhett that although I want to use antiques and reproductions, I don't want our home to look like a museum."

"Look around and if you like what you see, then I'll ask her if she's willing to look at your place."

"Thanks, brother love."

Xavier bowed gracefully from the waist. "You're quite welcome."

Selena opened the door to Sweet Persuasions, smiling at the couple who'd arrived promptly at three o'clock. Xavier had called earlier to tell her that he would direct them to the shop, but would not stay, because his sister and her fiancé planned to return to D.C. after they'd selected the design and filling for their wedding cake. The resemblance between Denise and Xavier was remarkable, she a delicately feminine version of her brother. Her fiancé was as classically handsome as her brother.

"Good afternoon. Welcome to Sweet Persuasions. I'm Selena Yates."

Denise returned the pastry chef's friendly smile. "Hi. I'm Denise."

Selena nodded. "And you must be Garrett," she said to the tall man standing behind his fiancée.

"Rhett," Garrett corrected, smiling.

Selena clasped her hands. "I've prepared more than a dozen fillings for you to sample. I also have a binder with a number of designs from which you can choose to decorate your cake. But if you have something specific in mind, then please let me know."

"Did my brother tell you we're going to marry in Philadelphia on New Year's Eve?"

"Yes."

"That won't be a problem?" Denise questioned.

Rhett rested a hand at the nape of his fiancée's neck. "Baby, if it was a problem we wouldn't be in Charleston, but talking to a pastry chef in D.C. or Philadelphia. Just let Ms. Yates do her job."

"Please sit down and we'll begin," Selena suggested. A stack of dessert plates with an ample supply of forks were on a nearby table. The countertop with the espresso machine was crowded with slices of cake, a different filling in each. "After you decide on the filling or fillings, then you must decide if you want to use a theme. You're getting married at the most festive time of the year, so perhaps you may want the decorations to reflect the holiday. Then there is the question of whether you want to cover the cake with butter cream, ganache, marzipan or royal icing."

Rhett seated Denise, then dropped down next to her. "What's the difference in the frostings?"

"Butter cream is a rich, whipped frosting made of butter, eggs and sugar. It can be flavored and used as a filling, frosting or piping decorations like flowers. Fondant is sugar dough that's rolled out into a smooth sheet, then smoothed over the cake. It's not easy to work with, but looks like porcelain and provides an ideal surface for decorating."

Selena took a breath. "Ganache is a combination of melted chocolate and cream and can be whipped to a consistency that can be used for filling or frosting. Royal icing is made of sugar and egg whites. It dries rock-hard when it hits the air. I use royal icing for piping flowers, borders and delicate scrolls.

"Marzipan is a doughy almond and sugar paste. It can be molded into shapes like fruits and can be rolled into sheets and draped over the cake like rolled fondant. Whipped cream is wonderful for fillings, too delicate for frostings. It doesn't pipe well and must be kept refrigerated. Any more questions before you start sampling?"

Denise nodded. "Can we have a different filling for each layer?"

"That's something I usually recommend when you have multiple layers," Selena said.

It took ninety minutes for Denise and Rhett to decide they wanted a four-tier cake with delicate, lacy piping on the sides of each layer. They also wanted pastillage flowers between the top two layers. There would be four small bouquets around the first layer and the topper would be flowers that matched Denise's bridal bouquet. They'd decided that the first layer would be filled with butter cream, the second with strawberry, the third with red velvet and the top carrot. Although both wanted a pistachio butter cream Denise had rejected it because she knew several guests had peanut allergies.

"I'll come to Philly the morning of your wedding and assemble the cake. If I need to make repairs, then that will give me enough time to complete it before the caterers arrive." She quickly computed the cost of the cake, while factoring in the expense of transporting it, and quoted a figure. Reaching into the breast pocket of his jacket, Rhett removed a case and handed her a card. Selena took the card, surprised by the weight of the square.

"It's made of carbon," Rhett explained when she held it in her palm.

"It's my first black card. I'll be right back."

Selena retreated to the rear of the shop where she'd set up the mini-office. She completed the computerized invoice, checking off items for the Eaton-Fennell wedding cake. Once she'd printed the invoice, she swiped Rhett's card.

She handed him back his card and an envelope with a copy of the invoice. Offering a smile and her hand, Selena said, "If I don't speak to you before, then I'll probably see you both on the day of your wedding."

"Are you staying for the wedding?" Rhett asked.

"No. I can't. I have a prior engagement."

Denise angled her head in a way that reminded Selena of Xavier. She still could not believe how much she had come to love him. It wasn't the frantic love that made her want to see and talk to him every waking minute of the day, but a relaxed uncomplicated love that was as quiet and predictable as a sunrise and sunset.

She enjoyed going shopping with him to buy things for his house. Selecting ceiling fans had taken on the gravity of balancing the budget for the city of Charleston. Every style she suggested Xavier rejected. It was when she accused him of not even remotely thinking of ceiling fans he'd turned on her like a snarling attack dog, saying he knew better than she what he wanted in his house.

Selena knew she'd shocked him when she'd turned on her heel and walked out of the store, while scrolling through her cell phone for the number for a taxi. Fortunately, there was a taxi letting off a passenger in the shopping center and she got in, gave the driver her address and returned home. She managed to cool down during the ride, but when her cell phone rang she refused to answer it when she saw Xavier's number. The calls continued for three days until on the fourth day she'd looked up to find him, in uniform, standing in front of the showcase at Sweet Persuasions. It was apparent he hadn't gone home to change but had come directly from school.

They'd engaged in a stare-down until he said the three words that melted her heart. His "I love you" was filled with so much emotion that she would've broken down if there hadn't been customers seated at the tables. She'd told him to come by later, and neither of them got much sleep that night. The makeup sex was beyond description, and she didn't remember whether Xavier had apologized, but that didn't matter as much the realization that he loved her as much as she loved him.

"If your plans change, then Rhett and I would be honored to have you there to celebrate our very special day."

"I'll definitely let you know if my plans do change."

Selena waited for Denise and Rhett to leave, then dimmed the lights and cleaned up everything. Today was Sunday, her day off but she'd gotten up very early to make the cake samples. She'd also made trays of Halloween cookies, several dozen caramel apples with nuts, sprinkles and shredded coconut and individual fruit pies. Individual servings were a favorite with most of her customers because it ensured portion control.

Reaching for her cell, she punched speed dial for Xavier. "Hey," she crooned when she heard his greeting. "I'm leaving now."

"Are you certain you don't want me to come and get you?"

"No, Xavier. Tomorrow is a holiday and I'm certain you want to sleep in late."

"I thought you were going to sleep in with me?"

Selena stared at the wall calendar. She had three special orders — one for Tuesday and the other two for Wednesday, and she wanted to set aside time to make the upcoming week's featured item: individual caramel-apple cake.

"Maybe I can work something out with my boss."

"Tell your boss that your man has planned something special for you."

"Hold on, Xavier, let me talk to her." She covered the mouthpiece with her thumb so he wouldn't hear her giggling. Selena moved her finger. "She said okay, only because she's a die-hard romantic."

"Remind me to send her a bouquet of flowers."

She giggled again. "Hang up, Xavier. I'll see you in about twenty minutes."

Xavier had accused Selena of keeping him off balance; however, she could've said the same when he led her blindfolded into the family room. "Am I going to like your surprise?"

Hands anchored around her waist, Xavier gently steered Selena over to a pile of pillows. "I'm going to help you sit down. Don't stiffen up on me, sweetheart. Let me do this. Now lean back."

Selena let her body go limp, slumping against Xavier as they sank downward. Instead of landing on the floor, she felt a cushion of pillows under her hips. Seconds later the blindfold was removed and she recognized the low cherrywood table with inset rosewood in a herringbone pattern. The table was set for two with china, silver and crystal. Votives in crystal holders flickered in the darkened space. An uncorked bottle of champagne sat in a bowl of ice and covered serving dishes were positioned at one end of the table.

Her gaze softened. "It's lovely. What are we celebrating?"

Pressing a button on a remote device, Xavier switched on a tuner, selecting the

MP3 feature. The melodious voice of Marc Anthony singing "Remember Me," filled the room as he sat on pillows beside Selena.

"We're celebrating our one-month anniversary."

She gave him a sidelong glance, marveling at the length of his lashes. "Why does it seem so much longer?"

"I don't know, babe. I feel as if I've known you for years."

Selena rested a hand on his back. "Not quite that long."

Xavier uncovered a dish with shrimp covered in a spicy sauce atop a bed of shredded lettuce, red cabbage, carrots and jicama. He uncovered another dish with an assortment of fish: prawns, clams on the half shell, lobster tails, smoked oysters and mussels.

Leaning to his left, he pressed a kiss on her hair. "Okay, a month. Give me your plate and I'll serve you."

Selena wanted to tell Xavier that six months ago she hadn't known he existed. She just opened Sweet Persuasions and every time the bell over the door rang her heart stopped while her stomach did a flip-flop. She knew people were curious about the sweets shop but she wasn't certain whether they would purchase the items she'd spent countless hours making not only edible but eye-appealing. Selena had begun to second-guess herself because of the pervasiveness of obesity ravaging the country. After two weeks she decided to offer smaller portions and business picked up. Smaller portions translated into less guilt.

Xavier filled the flutes with champagne, raising his in a toast. "Here's to the first of many more months, and very special congratulations to Sweet Persuasions for her upcoming television debut." He touched his glass to Selena's, winking and smiling at her over the rim.

Wrapped in a cocoon of contentment, Selena pressed her shoulder to Xavier's, feeding on his strength. If she had had a genie granting wishes for the perfect man, she definitely would've asked for someone like Xavier. She'd gotten over his terse remark about the ceiling fan, realizing if she hadn't walked away she would've said something that would have ended their relationship.

She'd grown up with a sharp tongue and quick temper, at times challenging her mother, but after losing privileges and being grounded she'd learned it was better to walk away than to argue with Geneva Yates.

"You know I'm a cheap date," she drawled

after her second glass of champagne.

"You're safe with me." Xavier's wine-scented breath feathered over her mouth when he angled his head. "I won't take advantage of you."

Her eyelids fluttered. "You promise?"

"I promise," he breathed out, seconds before taking possession of her mouth in a searing kiss that sucked the air from her lungs and leaving her feeling light-headed. "We should . . ." The telephone rang, preempting what he was going to say. His house phone rarely rang, and when it did it was usually a family member. "I have to answer that." Xavier reached over and picked up the cordless. "Hello."

"Xavier. Jimmy."

He smiled. "What's up?"

"Is Selena there with you? We tried calling her home and cell, but she didn't answer."

Xavier sobered. Why would Ellie's husband be looking for Selena? "Yes, she is. Why?"

There came a pause. "Someone broke into her shop. Whoever it was tripped the alarm and by the time my men got here they were gone. She needs to come and let us know if anything is missing."

"We're on our way."

He hung up, turned and found Selena

staring at him. "That was Jimmy McKinney. He called to say someone or something tripped your alarm at the shop. He wants you to come down and check to see if there is anything missing."

Selena didn't move for a full thirty seconds, and then she was galvanized into motion, reaching for her shoes. She prayed it was a false alarm, and if it wasn't she hoped someone hadn't burglarized Sweet Persuasions, because they would come up empty-handed. She never left money in the shop overnight, and during the day she kept enough on hand to make change. Her policy not to accept anything more than a fifty-dollar bill was strictly enforced, alleviating the need to have large sums of cash on hand.

Xavier was beside her when she picked up her handbag off the straight-back chair in the entryway, after he'd put out the candles. If she'd had to drive to the shop or come down from her apartment alone, Selena knew she would not have been so calm, because she could not fathom someone burglarizing Sweet Persuasions. There wasn't anything to steal — unless the thief was a chocoholic.

CHAPTER 15

Whoever had broken in had jimmied the back door. Fortunately, nothing was missing, but Selena still did not feel comfortable. The officers on the scene reported the door couldn't be dusted for prints until the following morning. She watched Xavier approach, offering him a forced smile.

Xavier cradled Selena's face. "I just called a locksmith. He should be here in about twenty minutes."

She wrapped her arms around his waist. "Thanks for being here."

"Where else would I be, Selena?"

"I don't know."

Xavier heard something in her voice he'd never heard before — fatigue. He hoped it was fatigue, not defeat. She'd worked nonstop to ensure business success but at what cost? Was what she'd hoped to achieve worth the risks it took to reach her goal?

He'd wanted to talk to Selena about it,

yet hadn't wanted her to think he didn't support her. When she'd told him about Derrick Perry, she'd complained that Perry had attempted to stifle her career when that wasn't what Xavier wanted. At twenty-six, Selena Yates had had not one, but two successful careers, but he wondered how long could she keep the same pace and not succumb to burnout. There was ambition, and there was also obsession.

A strident female voice came from the back door. Selena was instantly alert. "That's Monica. She's my neighbor," she explained, when Xavier gave her a questioning look. "Tell the police to let her in."

Seconds later Monica rushed inside with wide eyes. "I saw the lights from the police cruisers." She came to a complete stop when she saw Selena sitting at one of the tables, her head resting on folded arms. "What's going on?"

"Someone broke in through the back door," a deep voice said behind Monica.

Despite the gravity of the situation, Monica smiled at the man who'd seemingly won the heart of her friend. She'd only caught a cursory glance at him weeks ago, but seeing him up close and personal was still a visual treat. Selena had hit the jackpot.

"I'm Monica Mills. Selena and I are neighbors."

Xavier nodded at the petite woman with neatly twisted hair, wearing lounging pants and a T-shirt with a Disney character stamped on the front. "Hello, Monica. Xavier Eaton. I'm sorry we have to meet under these circumstances."

"Same here. Do the police know when it happened, because I've been home since two o'clock this afternoon and I didn't hear anything."

"I don't know," Xavier lied smoothly. The police didn't exactly say when they'd gotten the call that the alarm had been tripped, but because it was a part of an ongoing police investigation he didn't want to divulge that information.

Monica sat down next Selena. "Are you all right, girlfriend?"

Selena nodded. "I'm good. I'm trying to hold on to my last nerve."

Monica looked up at Xavier and told him about someone ringing the bell to Selena's apartment, and then not answering. "It could be they confused the shop with the rear entrance to our apartments."

Xavier pulled over another chair and straddled it. "Isn't the rear door to the apartments always locked?"

"Yes, but that doesn't stop people from walking past and trying it," Monica explained. "I've caught quite a few folks jiggling the lock. I don't know what they'd want other than perhaps they are nosy."

Xavier wanted to tell Monica *he* wasn't that naive. People tested doors to see if they were unlocked, and if they were it usually indicated an easy score. Why break in if you could walk in?

The locksmith arrived and promptly went to work replacing the lock. Monica returned to her apartment and her daughter and the police left, telling Selena she could pick up a copy of their report the following afternoon.

Selena had barely moved from the table where she'd sat listening to the conversations and activity going on around her. The enormity of the break-in had finally sunk it. Someone had violated her place of business — only steps from her home.

Xavier had settled the bill with the locksmith when she finally stood up. "I'm calling the security company tomorrow and having them install cameras."

"That's a good idea." Those were the last words Xavier said until they returned to his house.

Selena looked and acted robotic when she

told him she was going upstairs to shower before going to bed. He watched her climb the staircase. She appeared brittle enough to break into pieces if he'd touched her.

Xavier returned to the room where they'd celebrated their first-month anniversary and cleared away everything. He armed the security system, then climbed the staircase to the second floor. Selena mentioning the installation of cameras made him feel a lot more comfortable. If she'd had a more sophisticated security system she would've been able to capture the burglar on tape. He'd had cameras installed in and around his property, hoping and praying he would never have to encounter anyone breaking into his home.

Selena felt her knees shaking and she groped for the back of a chair to keep her balance. The technician who'd come out to install the minute cameras had asked whether the former tenant had installed a camera in the restroom, and her response was she didn't know.

The technician met Xavier's steely gaze. "There's not only a camera but a feed that's running upstairs."

Xavier's gaze swung from the man to Selena. "Is your apartment above the bathroom?" He'd asked the question though he knew the answer.

She nodded. "My bathroom is directly over the one down here. That's why it was so easy to install the bathroom because the pipes run along the same line."

"Do you want me to remove the wire?"

"Not yet," Xavier cautioned. "Wait until I call someone."

Selena gave him an incredulous look. "What do you mean not yet?"

Taking her arm, he led her a safe distance away so the technician couldn't overhear what he wanted to tell her. "Let me call someone at police headquarters. Whoever installed that camera and feeder wire has to be monitoring what is going on in both bathrooms. The only way they're going to catch this sick bastard is to trace where the signal is coming from."

"I have to use the bathrooms."

"No, you don't."

"I can't work all day without using the bathroom."

"Baby, please listen to me. You're going to put a sign on the door that the bathroom is out of order. If you need to use a bathroom, then ask Monica if she would let you use hers. Meanwhile, tell her there's something wrong with the pipes in the bathroom in your apartment and water is backing up down here."

Selena's eyes grew wide. "Why lie to her?"

"Someone installing cameras in public bathrooms is something that should handled by law enforcement."

"I can't impose on Monica when I want to use her bathroom at night or early in the morning."

"You're not going to impose on her, Selena. You're going to move in with me."

"No, no," she repeated. "I'm not going to live with you."

"You sleep with me, so —"

"I sleep with you, Xavier. That's very different from living with you."

"You have a problem living with me?"

"Lower your voice," Selena warned when the technician turned to stare at them. "I will not *shack up* with you." She'd enunciated the seven words.

"Would it make it better if we get married? Then we could live together without — as you call it — shacking up."

Selena's emotions vacillated between shock, anger, humiliation and confusion. The temper she'd managed to repress with maturity flared, spreading heat and rage as she went on tiptoe, thrusting her face close to Xavier's. "How dare you —"

"I dare, Selena," he countered. "I dare because I have a good reason to ask you to marry me. First, I love you. I've told you that so many times that I'm beginning to sound like a parrot. And because I do love you I want to protect and take care of you. I can't do that if you're going to put yourself in harm's way. Last, but certainly not least, why do you think I asked you to decorate the house? It certainly wasn't for me, because all I had to do was pick up the phone and call a local decorating firm. It's not my house but our house, baby. It's a place where we'll live and grow old together, but first we have to fill up a couple of those bedrooms with some babies."

Selena wanted to believe she'd imagined Xavier proposing to her, because somewhere in her subconscious it was something she'd wanted him to do. She'd fallen in love with him, wanting and praying he would be the man for her. What had stopped her from total commitment was the length of time in which they'd known each other. Yesterday they'd celebrated their one-month anniversary and knowing someone thirty days was not the basis or foundation on which she could consider a happily ever after.

"You're joking aren't you?" It was the first response that came to mind.

Xavier's expression had become a mask of stone. "Do I look like I'm joking?"

A beat passed. "No."

"Then what's it going to be? Yes or no?"

Selena wanted to ask him what he would do if she said no, but there was something in his eyes that said she would come to regret his answer or action. She loved Xavier, and she knew it was love and not infatuation because she'd never been in love. It wasn't often someone was offered a second chance at love, but she had been one of the luckier ones.

She took a step, pressing her breasts to his chest. "When do you want to do it?"

"What are you doing Thursday afternoon?"

Her mouth opened and closed several times as tears filled her eyes. "I'm not getting married at the courthouse."

"Where do you want to get married?"

"We can have the ceremony at the house. I'll ask the assistant pastor at the church where I go for Sunday services to officiate. If Monica doesn't have anything planned for Sunday, then she can be my witness. And if you want to invite your other friends, then we can have Emma Bell prepare the food."

Xavier suddenly saw his bride-to-be in a

whole new light. Now he knew why she ran a successful business. She was straightforward and confident. "I'll agree to whatever you want. I know you probably don't want to marry without having your family in attendance, but I promise to make it up to you."

The initial apprehensiveness Selena felt when Xavier proposed was missing, replaced by a gentle peace. "My family usually gets together for Thanksgiving. Do you think the Eatons can come to West Virginia for dinner and a wedding?"

Xavier smiled, lighting up his eyes. "Give them the date, time and place and they'll descend on your people like locusts."

"You have to let me know how many are coming because I'll call a hotel and have them set aside a block of rooms."

Pulling her close, he pressed a kiss to her forehead. "I'll handle the Eatons and you take care of the Yateses. I'm not going to tell anyone until after we're married, only because I don't want to deal with my mother's histrionics. Whatever you decide to do with your family is all right with me."

"We'll tell them together."

Xavier kissed her again. "Let me call the police and tell them about the camera. They'll know how to handle it. Meanwhile, the techie can install cameras everywhere but the bathroom."

Selena nodded numbly like a bobblehead doll, not wanting to think of what she'd just agreed to. Within a span of a month, her life had been turned upside down, righted, then turned sideways. And, within another month, with her family in attendance, she would repeat her vows in a ceremony with a man who'd swept into her life like the force of an EF5 twister, sweeping up everything in its wake.

Selena stood under the large tent in the garden with Xavier, gazing lovingly into his eyes when he repeated his vows. It was her twenty-seventh birthday *and* her wedding day. There was no way Xavier could ever forget their wedding anniversary.

The weather had decided to cooperate with temperatures in the mid-seventies and warm southerly breezes stirring the skirt of her oyster-white, Victorian-style slip-dress. The dress matched the pumps she'd purchased from a shop featuring vintage clothing. Leandra had styled her hair in a mass of tiny curls that moved every time she turned her head.

The gathering that had started with a dozen guests had swelled to nearly thirty when Xavier invited several Christopher Munroe Academy instructors and their wives to witness their nuptials. Tantalizing smells wafted from dishes set up at the opposite end of the tent where guests would avail themselves of a low-country buffet of a plethora of dishes ranging from popping fried shrimp, fried spareribs, chicken, barbecued pig feet, chitlins, snap beans with potatoes, butter beans, potato salad, macaroni and cheese, hoppin' John, okra, seafood rice and red rice with spicy sausage. In lieu of a wedding cake, Selena had fashioned a pyramid of chocolate cupcakes with a variety of frostings and toppings. She'd planned to make the traditional wedding cake for her Thanksgiving wedding.

They exchanged rings, the minister pronounced them man and wife, followed by a kiss to seal their troth, and it was over. She was now Mrs. Selena Yates-Eaton. They'd discussed her retaining her maiden name because of Sweet Persuasions.

She and Xavier spent hours talking about what they wanted for their future. He would accept a full-time teaching position at the academy at the beginning of the next school year, and in March she would go completely mail order. Selena had decided not to renew her lease on her apartment or the shop, putting the furniture and whatever she didn't need at the present time in storage. Xavier had conferred with his architect who would draw up plans to expand one side of the house for a commercial kitchen from which she would operate Sweet Persuasions and the opposite side for a guest cottage. What they hadn't agreed on was when to start a family. They had given themselves the end of the year on which to make a decision.

"Ladies and gentlemen, I'm honored to present Mr. and Mrs. Xavier Eaton." The minister's sonorous voice resounded in the tent like a megaphone.

Enthusiastic applause filled the tent as Selena and Xavier turned to face those who'd come to witness one of the momentous days in their lives. Bending slightly, he pressed a kiss to Monica Mills's daughter's cheek. Selena had selected her to stand in as the flower girl.

"How did you get so beautiful?" he whispered.

A becoming blush suffused the eight-year-old's gold-brown face framed by a wealth of reddish curls. She'd inherited her petite body from Monica, but her large hazel eyes and features were her father's. Trisha lowered her gaze and Xavier was enchanted by the gesture. He'd thought about having a son, but there was something about Monica's daughter that made his heart ache each time he saw her. Yes, he wanted a daughter, a little girl who was the image of Selena.

"I don't know."

Sweeping her up in his arms, Xavier carried her around as he and Selena personally thanked everyone for coming. If Selena was her auntie, then he would become the child's uncle.

The one person he hadn't expected to see walked into the tent. James McKinney hadn't been able to switch with another officer, so Ellie had come without him. Jimmy, who was in uniform, stopped to kiss his wife, then beckoned for Xavier.

He set Trisha on her feet. "Uncle Xavier will see you later," Xavier said with Jimmy's approach. He and the police officer exchanged a rough hug. "Thanks for stopping by."

Jimmy angled his head, smiling. "You look comfortable in civvies." The tailored dark gray suit, white silk and platinum tie and black wingtips were perfect for an informal wedding.

"I'm getting used to them."

Resting a hand on Xavier's shoulder Jimmy lead him away from the crowd lining up at the buffet. "I came by to tell you we turned the case over to the feds. Our techie discovered the camera feed originates on the West Coast."

Xavier's eyes narrowed. "Where exactly on the West Coast?"

"He believes in or around L.A. The experts at the Bureau will definitely come up with the pervert who installed that camera."

Xavier hadn't felt comfortable with Selena working in the shop alone. However, with the cameras in and outside Sweet Persuasions, and everyone having to be buzzed in and out had lessened some of his anxiety.

"Can you stay long enough to eat?"

The lines around Jimmy's brown eyes fanned out when he flashed a wide grin. "Why do you think I came by during my dinner hour?"

Xavier slapped his back. "Eat up. There's more than enough food."

Bobby Bell came over to join them. Xavier had chosen Bobby as his best man. "You staying, Jimmy?"

The police officer shook his head. "Just long enough to fill my belly."

"Sorry, but Mama Bell didn't make no donuts," Bobby teased.

"You keep messin' with me Bobby and I'm going to give you a mess of citations for that raggedy-ass hoopty you can't seem to part with."

Bobby threw back his head and laughed. "You're just jealous cause I bought your truck and rebuilt it so it runs like new."

"I'll see you boys later," Xavier threw over his shoulder. It was time he got back to his wife.

Thanksgiving Day
Mingo County, West Virginia

Selena felt like Alice in Wonderland. She hadn't fallen down a rabbit hole. She'd entered the barn, which had been transformed into a fairyland setting with countless tiny white lights, long tables covered with orange and brown tablecloths and bales of hay stacked against the wall. Cornstalks in baskets stood like sentinels and vases with autumnal flowers as centerpieces, on the arm of her husband.

She and Xavier had exchanged vows a second time at the tiny church where she had been baptized and had attended services every Sunday of her childhood. The exception was when she was too sick to get out of bed, or a snowstorm made roads impassible.

"Oh, my goodness!"

She wasn't able to conceal her amazement. Her mother, grandmother and sistersin-law had outdone themselves. When she'd arrived in Matewan the day before Thanksgiving the women in her family had insisted she relax and do nothing more than breathe.

Xavier wrapped his arm around the waist of his twice-wed wife over the silk-and-satin wedding gown that kissed her slender body like a caress. When he'd married her in Charleston she had been a woman-child with the slip dress and curly hairstyle, but now she was all woman in Matewan with her hair brushed off her face. Jeweled pins tucked into the coil of her hair, from which flowed a veil in tulle that matched the pearl-and-diamond earrings in her pierced lobes. He'd exchanged his suit for a tuxedo, gray vest, black-and-gray-striped tie and stark, white shirt.

He glanced up at the loft stacked with bales of hay. It'd rained earlier that morning and the sweet smell from the dried grass hung in the crisp, cool air. "If it wasn't for the hay, you'd never believe this was a barn." Xavier had always wanted to visit historic Matewan, but he could not have imagined it would be as the husband of a woman whose family's roots spanned more than a century in the coal-mining region.

Close to one hundred people rose and applauded as "Time of My Life" blared from the speakers resting on bales of hay in the loft. Reaching for his wife's right hand, Xavier spun her around the straw-littered floor. Within seconds couples were up on their feet singing and dancing to the upbeat song from the *Dirty Dancing* soundtrack.

Selena leaned closer, pressing her mouth to Xavier's ear. "I thought the tradition was the bride and groom dance together, then she with her father and he with his mother."

Xavier swung her around and around. "We're hardly traditional, baby. Remember, we were married when we arrived."

She pressed closer to his body. "Married and free."

The FBI had identified Derrick Perry as the one who'd had the camera installed in Sweet Persuasions's bathroom. The computer geek he'd paid to fuel his perversions rolled over when a U.S. Attorney threatened to charge him with cyber-stalking, child pornography and invasion of privacy and that he would have to register as a sex offender because some of the pictures were of young children. The frightened young man sang like the proverbial canary and Derrick's father could only stand by and watch as special agents handcuffed his son, read him his Miranda rights and took him to jail.

"Perry never would've been able to track you if he hadn't known your legal name. But, it all worked out because you were only one of several women he'd stalked using concealed cameras."

She pulled back to meet Xavier's eyes. "I just hope I'm not called on to testify, because I don't think I'd be able to sit in the same room with him."

He swung her out, then pulled her close to his chest. "You may not have to if he decides to take a plea. If not, then I'll have to decide how I'm going to get close enough to him to beat him to a bloody pulp."

Selena frowned. "Now you sound like Luke, who promised to stomp a mud hole in his behind."

"I believe the word is *ass,* darling. And spoken like a jarhead."

Her eyebrows lifted. "That's the first time I've ever heard you refer to a marine as a jarhead."

Xavier was saved from replying when an elderly woman tapped him on the arm. "Do you mind if I cut in?"

"Grandma!"

Lily Yates glared at her only granddaughter. "Don't Grandma me. You have the rest of your life to dance with this young man, and I only have the weekend to find out if he's worthy of my grandbaby girl."

Selena stepped back, turned and bumped into an immovable object. She looked up to find Kenyon Chandler staring at her. Every normal woman in Mingo County had tried to get her cousin to either go out with them or lure him into their bed. But the quiet, serious lawman appeared totally oblivious to their advances. Selena knew he liked women — just the ones who didn't throw their panties at him.

She held out her arms and she wasn't disappointed when he placed a hand at her waist and took her right hand with the other. If Xavier was eye candy, then Kenyon was off-the-charts gorgeous.

"Is it true you're thinking of running for sheriff once my father announces his retirement?"

Kenyon shook his head, his dark gray eyes staring at something over her shoulder. "That's nothing more than gossip. I like where I am."

When he spun her around Selena realized who her cousin had been staring at. It was Mia Eaton. The tall elegant Dallas woman had flown in earlier that morning with her family. She'd mistaken her for a high-fashion model until Xavier introduced her as Dr. Eaton.

"Do you like what you see, cousin?" she teased.

"She's pretty. But she's also stuck up."

"Why would you say that?"

"Look at the way she's looking down her nose at us."

Selena stopped in the middle of the dance floor. "Would you like me to introduce you to her?"

"No," Kenyon said, much too quickly. "I have no problem meeting my own women." That said, he escorted Selena over to the table where her parents sat, turned on his heels and walked out of the barn.

Selena lost track of how many times she had been asked to dance. She managed to stop long enough to eat a few bites of what had become a Thanksgiving feast. The Eatons outnumbered the Yates two-to-one, but what the Yates lacked in numbers they more than made up for with enthusiasm.

After numerous toasts and long-winded speeches, she and Xavier managed to slip away, changing behind the partition of the limousine as the chauffeur drove across the state line to Kentucky for their second wedding night.

This wedding night would differ from their first. They'd decided not to wait to start a family. Hopefully when they celebrated their first wedding anniversary it would be as parents of a son or daughter.

ABOUT THE AUTHOR

Rochelle Alers has been hailed by readers and booksellers alike as one of today's most prolific and popular African American authors of romance and women's fiction.

With more than sixty titles and nearly two million copies of her novels in print, Ms. Alers is a regular on the Waldenbooks, Borders and *Essence* bestseller lists, regularly chosen by Black Expressions Book Club, and has been the recipient of numerous awards, including a Gold Pen Award, an Emma Award, a Vivian Stephens Award for Excellence in Romance Writing, an *RT Book Reviews* Career Achievement Award and a Zora Neale Hurston Literary Award.

Ms. Alers is a member of the Iota Theta Zeta Chapter of Zeta Phi Beta Sorority, Inc., and her interests include gourmet cooking and traveling. She has traveled to

Europe and countries in North, South and Central Americas. Her future travel plans include visits to Hong Kong and New Zealand. Ms. Alers is also accomplished in knitting, crocheting and needlepoint. She is currently taking instruction in the art of hand quilting.

Oliver, a toy Yorkshire terrier, has become the newest addition to her family. When he's not barking at passing school buses, the tiny dog can be found sleeping on her lap while she spends hours in front of the computer. A full-time writer, Ms. Alers lives in a charming hamlet on Long Island.

The employees of Thorndike Press hope you have enjoyed this Large Print book. All our Thorndike, Wheeler, and Kennebec Large Print titles are designed for easy reading, and all our books are made to last. Other Thorndike Press Large Print books are available at your library, through selected bookstores, or directly from us.

For information about titles, please call:

(800) 223-1244

or visit our Web site at:

http://gale.cengage.com/thorndike

To share your comments, please write:

Publisher
Thorndike Press
10 Water St., Suite 310
Waterville, ME 04901